"I never eat when I get on a cooking kick."

"Well, hell, that's no

"No, I um…no." Sh
wanted her hands in
sported.

"Is that because there
upset?"

She opened the refrigerator door and then closed it. "There's no one."

"Does *he* know that?"

Setha blinked and turned from the refrigerator to study him curiously. "What are you talking about?"

Khouri maintained his spot along the counter. "You're starting to offend me. Turning down all my invitations."

She resumed wiping down the countertops, starting with the one nearest him. "You'll get over it," she grumbled.

"Don't be so sure," he said, moving from the counter and turning her against it.

He'd moved so quickly, she'd barely had time to register the change in her position. The only thing registering then was his mouth on hers. He delivered the kiss thoroughly, enticing her tongue into the sultriest of duels. Infrequently, he curved his tongue over and around hers and then traced the even ridge of her teeth, which coaxed her to do the same to him.

"What are you doing?" She barely formed the words when he finally let her up for air.

"Giving you what you wanted earlier."

Books by AlTonya Washington

Kimani Romance

ALTONYA WASHINGTON

has been a published romance novelist of contemporary and historical fiction for eight years. Her novel *Finding Love Again* won the *RT Book Reviews* Reviewers' Choice Award for Best Multicultural Romance in 2004. In addition to teaching a community-college course entitled *Writing the Romance Novel*, she works as a senior library assistant, resides in North Carolina and is currently working to obtain her master's in library science. Writing as T. Onyx, AlTonya releases erotic romance. Her latest release with the Harlequin/Kimani label was the January 2012 title *Pleasure After Hours.* She will release the twelfth installment in her popular Ramsey/Tesano series, *A Lover's Hate,* in 2012.

TEXAS LOVE Song

AlTonya Washington

Love and thanks to my family for being so patient
when I spend so much time writing.

Recycling programs
for this product may
not exist in your area.

ISBN-13: 978-0-373-86265-8

TEXAS LOVE SONG

Copyright © 2012 by AlTonya Washington

For questions and comments about the quality of this book, please contact us
at Customer_eCare@Harlequin.ca.

www.Harlequin.com

Printed in U.S.A.

Dear Reader,

You've decided to embark upon a mystery and witness the unfolding of a romance. *Texas Love Song* is a fitting title for this story. The relationship between Khouri Ross and Setha Melendez was crafted to possess the beauty, longing and desire of the ballads we adore. Khouri and Setha come into each other's lives amid dark circumstances, which are the key to a mystery that affects their families.

It was challenging and rewarding to craft a complex suspense within the allure of a love story. Those of you who know my work know that I delight in mixing these elements. It was also very exciting and quite fitting to create larger-than-life characters who hail from the bold state of Texas. I hope you'll enjoy the effort and tune in for its companion piece, *His Texas Touch,* in August. Please email your thoughts to altonya@lovealtonya.com.

Blessings,

Al

Prologue

She could've celebrated the loss of those killer pumps had she lost them anywhere besides a dark alley. Unfortunately, it was either lose the shoes or give herself away to the creep who'd been following her all night. She knew of course that he'd been stalking her much longer than that.

Setha Melendez gave another quick glance across her shoulder and felt momentary ease when no shadow passed in her line of sight.

Son of a b, she hissed silently, wisps of dark hair fluttering beneath her nostrils as she inhaled deeply to catch her breath. She cursed her pursuer again for involving them in this when it had nothing to do with them. None of it had been their fault.

Setha grimaced; those words sounded naive even though they'd been spoken silently in her head. There was one thing she'd learned at an early age. In the Melendez family, it was one for all and all for one. If one was despised, they all were.

Her quick breather reached its end when the clatter of a rolling bottle caught her ear. The sound had come from the far end of the alley. Setha cast a last, longing look at the awesome pumps and then figured she'd better get a move on. She prayed whoever found her discarded shoes had more fun wearing them than she did.

"Jumpin' ship already, man?" Bose Osmond grinned at his boss's older brother.

Khouri Ross returned the grin while shaking hands with Bose who was one of the seven bouncers at his sister's club. "I'll leave you and your colleagues to it," he said, casting a weary hazel stare at the bodies packing the three-story brick building. "Never been a fan of love songs." He shrugged.

"Understood." Bose nodded solemnly from his perch guarding the club's back entrance. "Rocky says she's tryin' to soften the club's image."

Khouri chuckled. "In *this* neighborhood?"

Bose joined in on the laughter at Raquel Ross's expense. The chuckles shaking his large frame ended on a sigh and he scratched the smattering of whiskers covering his chin. "So how's Avra doin'?"

"Still mean." Khouri shook his head at the mention of his older sister.

"Still fine?" Bose's question was laced with interest.

The look on the man's face instilled more laughter in Khouri. Amusement crinkled the corners of his translucent stare. "You're a glutton for punishment, B."

Bose raised one hand as though he were about to

testify. "What can I say? A woman like that can make a man do anything."

"Hmph. Don't I know it," Khouri groaned while patting his sagging dark jeans for keys. It was because of Avra that he'd been checking up on their little sister and her club that night. While he was most definitely a protective older brother, he'd have rather spent the night at his monthly poker game.

"See ya around, B." Khouri clutched Bose's hand for a quick shake and hug, and then left through the rear VIP entrance to Rocky Ross's.

Khouri's phone chimed just as he approached the black Rover bearing the personalized plates carrying his first name. There was a text from Niko Latham, one of his poker buddies. The man had wasted no time boasting about his winnings from the night and thanked Khouri for his absence.

Smirking, Khouri opened the passenger door to the Rover. Dropping down to the leather champagne-colored seat, he texted back telling Niko to enjoy his one and only win. Then he stood to ease the phone into a side pocket when he lost his balance as someone brushed against him.

Lengthy hair and a gasping sound gave him pause but didn't slow his reflexes. He caught the woman's forearm and held her fast.

"Calm down," he whispered, tilting his head to get a look at her face partially covered by thick black tendrils. He could see that she was terrified. "I won't hurt you," he said.

The woman struggled viciously and her gaze remained fixed on the alley she'd just run out of.

Soon, Khouri's light eyes were trained in that direction, as well. "Someone's following you?"

"Please." Her tugs against his hold lost some of their power. She had yet to look away from the alley.

"Let's go inside." Again, Khouri shifted his head to get a better look at her face—a beautiful one at that.

The woman shook her head frantically and slightly renewed her struggles against his hold.

Khouri opened the passenger door to the Rover. "At least have a seat in my car while I get some help."

She tugged more insistently on the imprisoned arm. With her free hand, she kept a death grip on the clutch purse at her chest. Still, her eyes remained on the darkness filling the alley.

"Please?" It was Khouri's turn to urge. He eased his grip on her wrist and motioned toward the passenger seat.

Eventually, the woman shifted her gaze. She didn't appear any more trusting of the seat than she did of the faceless threat in the distance. When noise rose from the alleyway, she chose the lesser of two evils and took refuge in the SUV.

She'd slammed the door shut before Khouri could do the honors. She used the flaring sleeves of her mocha-colored swing dress to cover the lower half of her face. Khouri watched her slink down in the seat, appearing every bit the timid child. The windows were tinted a few shades above complete black, but she remained hunched low.

Khouri told himself to focus on the matter at hand and he reached for his phone. He was about to dial inside the club for someone to come outside, when the sound of a runner caught his ears. Eyes narrowed toward the dark alleyway beyond the club, he waited. He winced, feeling a dull pressure tighten his palms. He realized his hands were aching to reach out and instill the same fear that the man running toward him had instilled in the woman who cowered in his car.

Somehow, he resisted the urge. The hooded pursuer raced by the other side of the Rover. Silence returned to the alley as the figure ran farther into the distance.

Khouri turned, intending to help the woman from his car. Again, the woman handled the door herself. Jumping out to the sidewalk, she sprinted off in the opposite direction from her tracker.

"You're welcome," Khouri said to her departing figure.

Chapter 1

The *Ross Review* boasted offices out of Miami, New York and London. The publication was headquartered in Houston, Texas, and was the brainchild of Louisiana native Basil Ross. The man had become a household name among a host of literary circles.

At eighteen, Basil—along with his childhood friend Wade Cornelius—started the weekly publication from the laundry room next to his mother's in-home hair salon. Back then, the magazine was geared toward Basil's peers. Topics covered the various challenges facing the black population in '60s-era Louisiana.

Reporting from a purely militant viewpoint, the *Review* was of course underground in nature. Basil realized the dangers in reporting on civil inequality and racial attacks on the national, state and local levels. Still, he thrived in the knowledge of that very thing.

The young publisher had made a name for himself long before he ever decided to put down stakes in Texas.

Upon visiting the *Review,* one would take the news floor as anything but. There was however a cool efficiency about the place. Reporters and staff toiled away at neat, high-end polished oak desks and were surrounded by glass walls in addition to windows.

Big-screen plasma TVs hung from various points in the ceiling on most every floor and broadcasted news from twenty-four-hour stations. The stations were also part of the *Ross Review* umbrella which, in the mid-nineties, had been added to Basil Ross's list of accomplishments.

While *Ross Review* employees were privy to an enviable view of downtown Houston, those on the other side of the glass had no clue about the goings-on of the organization inside. The underlying reason for the one-way windows was clear and spoke to the publication's motto. *Ross would reveal no "crime" before its time.*

The overall effect of the eighteen-story building may have come across as cold, stark and uninviting but Basil Ross treated his employees very well. Editorial and custodial staff alike was given the utmost respect. Proof was evident in their working conditions and compensation. Basil Ross and Wade Cornelius each subscribed to the notion that a well-treated worker was an effective worker.

Aside from the drone of voices rising from the TVs, there was minimal personal chatter. Everyone was about his or her business and proud to be. Anyone privileged enough to walk through the doors of the *Ross Review* understood that they were walking into the environment of respect and admiration the publication waved like a banner.

* * *

Inside one of the glass-encased conference rooms, the dull rumble of laughter could be heard as the daily budget meeting began to wind down. Basil made a point of ending every meeting on a cordial note. The issues reported on by the magazine and stations were often so melancholy, smiles were hard to come by unless a story brought a criminal to justice.

Such was the case that morning. A dual effort between the crime and financial beats had yet to fully uncover the true motive behind a series of murders targeting new Machine Melendez employees.

"Follow the money, boys," Basil was saying to his chief reporters for each beat. "You've already uncovered that the murders were professionally done. That costs money." He watched David Crus and Noah Eames nod solemnly as he smiled.

"Show me you're worth what I'm paying you," Basil added, drawing a round of laughter in the process.

"Speaking of money," Basil started once the chuckles began to silence. He reached for the last folder to his left and grimaced upon opening it. "I regret to announce that change will need to be made with regards to the Machine Melendez account." Pulling the silver-rimmed spectacles from his nose, Basil focused on wiping the already spotless lenses. "Apologies for bringing noneditorial business into our budget meeting but since our two VPs are right here…"

Basil replaced the square-framed glasses and looked toward his son and daughter at the end of the table. "It's best to get this out of the way now. I don't want this mess fouling up the rest of my day."

Avra Ross lowered her brown gaze while scooting

down a bit in her chair. Squeezing the cup in hand, she focused on blowing across the surface of her coffee in order to cool it. She looked up when her father loudly cleared his throat.

"You're gonna owe your brother big for this one, miss," he said.

Blinking, Avra cast a quick look toward Khouri. She looked away just as quickly when he sent her a smug grin.

"You may not be so pleased when you find out what she's gonna owe you for, sir."

Khouri's grin showed signs of dimming just a tad. Reclining in his chair, he stroked the light beard shadowing his face and waited.

"Too many negatives appear to be plaguing this account." Basil perched his slender frame to the edge of the table. "Foremost is the fact that the lead execs can't pass a civil word between the two of them."

"The man's a pig," Avra grumbled, once more staring into her coffee.

Basil leaned toward his eldest child. "And you're saying that you've never played nice with pigs before?"

"Not with pigs that big." Avra smiled when laughter rumbled around the table. She cleared her throat upon noticing Basil's dry expression.

"With that in mind, it's time for cooler heads to prevail." He looked from Avra who was easing down deeper into her chair. "Khouri, the job is yours."

Khouri's enviable, laid-back demeanor showed the slightest signs of unrest. "Dad, um." He slanted a look toward his sister. "I don't have a clue about what Av and her crew do over there in advertising. I'm not ashamed to say I don't know about negotiating ad rates, either."

"Understood, sir." Basil smiled approvingly when his only son smirked over his use of the pet name. His expression tightened once more when he again looked toward his daughter. "But this isn't about ad rates, is it, miss?"

Indignant, Avra set down her extra-tall coffee cup and folded her hands atop the table. "We don't think Melendez's proposed spots are right for the magazine," she told her brother.

Khouri pressed a hand to the front of the gray shirt he wore. "And you think *I'd* know which are right?"

"We're hoping your input might help us reach a decision for everyone to be happy," Basil said, looking through the papers inside the folder he referred to. "We want to remove this from the ad department completely. Basically, we don't want any of Avra's staff feeling pressured into doing her bidding instead of sharing their true opinions."

Avra bristled. "Dad—"

"Is Melendez all right with this?" Khouri smoothly interjected.

"They are sending their own cooler head to assist."

Khouri realized the futility in asking more questions. The job, as his father said, was all his. The look he sent Avra then should have left no doubts that he was pissed and that she definitely owed him big time.

Basil slid the folder down the long table. "Someone from Melendez will call to set up a meeting."

A knock fell upon the conference room door just as discussion resumed among the group. Basil's assistant, Doris Shipman, hurried in. She whispered briefly near her boss's ear, pressed a slip of paper into his hand and left the room.

Opening the note, Basil scanned the writing. His expression changed as he leaned forward and drew the strip of paper closer.

"Everything okay, Dad?" Avra shared a concerned look with Khouri when their father simply raised a hand and rushed from the room.

Samson Melendez smoothed the back of one hand along his square jaw and studied the young woman seated on the other side of his desk. Through a narrowed, dark gaze he focused intently on her face looking for anything to disprove what she was telling him.

"Convinced?" Setha Melendez asked her brother after he'd silently watched her for the better part of two minutes.

"Not really." Sam's canyon-deep voice had the tendency to fill a room especially when his words carried the added air of suspicion. "I can't understand anyone— who's in their right mind—volunteering to spend hours negotiating with the likes of Avra Ross."

Setha recrossed her long legs. "No one except you, right?" she drawled, smiling brightly when her brother's probing-pitch stare wavered. She elected not to call him on it. "Anyway, I won't be dealing with Avra but with her brother."

"Khouri?" Samson pushed out of the hulking desk chair that was set behind an equally massive desk. "He's no adman. He's his dad's right-hand guy. This is a little below his pay grade."

"Well, apparently he doesn't think so." Setha bit down on her bottom lip in an attempt to douse her smile. The times were few and far between when anyone managed to surprise Samson Melendez. She swung her foot a bit more merrily. The moment was definitely one to be savored.

Samson took a seat on the corner of his desk and fixed his little sister with another probing glare. "Why wasn't I told about this, Set?"

Still savoring the moment, Setha shrugged and studied the fringe hemline of the tan wrap dress she wore. "If I had to guess, it'd probably be because the decision had already come down from the top."

Sam leaned forward a bit. "Dad?"

"Mmm...and Basil Ross."

Sam winced then. "Old fools," he muttered, running a hand across his dark, straight hair. "They haven't got a clue about advertising."

"But they do have a clue about getting things done." Setha leaned forward then to pin her brother with a teasing leer. "I guess they figure since you and Avra Ross have issues..."

"Bullshit." Sam began to massage his forehead. "I got no issues with that woman aside from bein' aggravated out of my mind every time I see her."

"Mmm..." Setha propped fist to chin and wondered if Sam had any idea of how soft his voice had become.

Obviously he did for his gaze narrowed in renewed suspicion. "You asked for this, didn't you?" He coolly shifted the subject.

The smug expression on Setha's licorice-dark face showed the slightest traces of unease then. Aside from being hard to surprise, her brother had a scary talent for reading people. "Dad asked me to step in," she blurted and stood from her chair. "He thought I'd like a change of pace since we're a bit slow just now," she added, referring to her job managing Melendez Corporate Charities.

"Bullshit again," Sam said while folding his arms over his chest. "Why the hell would you want to be involved in this?"

"I wanted to help."

"Double bullshit." Sam gave her the benefit of a hard stare for only a few seconds longer and then shrugged. "But I won't argue."

"I promise I'm not after your job, Sam." Setha clutched her hands to the center of her chest. "Besides, I don't know a thing about negotiating ad rates."

"Then you're in luck since *rates* aren't what we can't agree on." He leaned across the massive desk and grabbed a hefty file there. He passed it to Setha and waved a hand to urge her to view its contents.

Obliging, Setha peered into the worn folder and scanned the first 8½x11 glossy she picked up. Her mouth fell open. "You're not serious?"

Khouri adjourned the budget meeting following his father's hasty departure. He forbade Avra to leave and grilled her about the advertising issue being unsettled with a client because of personal differences. Avra, unfortunately, wasn't interested in discussing the Melendez account.

"Did you see how he just rushed out?" She bit her thumbnail while watching the closed conference room door.

"So what?" Khouri didn't break his slow stride while pacing the room and shuffling through the account folder.

Avra rolled her eyes. *"So what?"*

"Hell, Av, he's gotten notes and had to leave meetings early before."

Avra's gaze slid back to the door. "There's more to it. He looked strange… I don't think I've ever seen that look on his face before, have you? Khouri?"

Her brother didn't respond and Avra waited for him to pass by during his pacing. She reached out to punch his arm and winced when her fist connected with an iron-hard bicep. "Dammit, Khouri, the least you can do is listen to me."

Khouri's deep-set stare was focused on his mobile. "Your client wants a meeting in the morning," he muttered. "They're sending Setha Melendez."

Avra's brows rose and her expression turned animated. "Aah…the baby sis—they really *are* going after cooler heads. Prettier heads, too."

"Pretty." Khouri smirked over his sister's use of the word.

"Haven't you ever met her?" Avra folded her arms across the tailored salt-and-pepper vest she sported. "I was sure that you had…."

Khouri only shook his head.

"Guess that makes sense. Hmph, she's not a big presence at the company—works for the charity end, handling money the corporation donates internationally or somethin' like that." She rolled her eyes and eased from her perch on the table. "If what I've heard from most men is true, then you're in for a real treat tomorrow morning."

Khouri remained silent and Avra guessed—*hoped*—he was too preoccupied by the upcoming meeting to worry over her departure. She took advantage of the fact and decided to try for a quiet escape.

Answering the email regarding the meeting, Khouri didn't lift his head. "We're not done yet," he called.

"Damn, Khouri…" Avra was seconds away from stomping her feet in agitation. "Sam Melendez's idea of advertising auto parts is to have some half-naked woman cradling brake pads between her boobs. Now I don't think that's what we want on the pages of the *Review,* do you?"

"Maybe not." Khouri chuckled while finishing up with the email. "But it'd sure as hell sell a crap load of brake pads."

"Khouri…" She actually whined that time.

Grinning, Khouri agreed that he'd hounded his big sister long enough. "I need for you to send me everything you've got on this thing so I won't look like a complete fool for the Melendez's prettier head."

"Deal. As soon as I check in on Dad."

Khouri eased the phone into his trouser pocket. "Do you honestly think there's anything to be upset about?"

"I hope not." She shrugged and extended her hand. "Care to join me and find out?"

Chapter 2

Setha refused to take an office at Machine Melendez. After all, she really was there only to offer her assistance with the advertising issue. At least it was the *issue* that gave her the opportunity she needed to get inside *Ross Review*.

While the man she needed to see was no longer associated with the publication, the advertising angle would *hopefully* give her the chance to get a feel for the Ross family. Basil Ross especially. She knew how it felt to be wrongly perceived by someone she'd never met.

Sighing, she curved her bare feet beneath her on the rust-colored suede sofa in Samson's office and reviewed the portfolio he'd given her.

"Better take a stab at educating myself on this so the man won't think I'm a complete idiot," Setha murmured, thinking of her meeting with Khouri Ross.

She couldn't help but laugh as she browsed the

glossy artwork for the proposed Machine Melendez ads in the *Ross Review*. No wonder Avra Ross couldn't work with Sam, she thought. In her brother's defense, however, Setha knew he was only seeing dollars and not…well…sex. It was yet another testament to how well he read people. He knew what would sell. That, in addition to the fact that *Machine* Melendez could have easily been called *Macho* Melendez.

Setha smiled at the thought. While her brothers were a handful, she was happy that her father had been blessed with three sons to immerse in the world of men. Daughters would have definitely not fared well, but her dad would have certainly tried to…initiate them.

Setha harbored no jealousy or envy toward her brothers. She was quite pleased with being the "softer side" of the Melendez clan. At least, she was quite pleased with letting the men in her life *think* she was the softer side. They would hit the roof if they knew what she'd been up to over the past several months.

She had to admit they'd have a right to hit the roof. Only to herself could she admit that she'd gotten in way over her head. But then, wasn't that the Melendez way? Get in deep, be so driven to succeed that it was necessary to fight to get out from beneath it all? And yet, be better for it because of the struggle?

Setha cast aside the artwork and groaned, wearily massaging a stockinged foot. It had been forty-eight hours since the night she'd literally had to run for her life. Whoever her pursuer was, he was no fool. He had seemed to anticipate her moves before she even made them.

Or, perhaps he had help? Setha shook her head to cast off the even more unsettling possibility. Nervously, she twirled a wayward onyx-colored tendril about her index finger. How had the simple act of helping someone turned into the equivalent of opening a can of worms? The more she'd dug for answers—the deeper she'd gotten—the more she'd discovered and the news wasn't good.

Could her father have really been involved in what she'd discovered? True, most businesses as widespread and lucrative as Machine Melendez often owed its success to a foundation of ugliness but her father, Danilo, was not a ruthless man.

Resting her head on the sofa back, she shut out the voice that revised the statement. *Danilo Melendez was not a ruthless father.* Setha knew full well that the man's business prowess was in fact ruthless to say the least.

She wasn't involved in the business to the same extent as her brothers, but Setha was aware of her father's tactics. Strong-arming landowners to obtain property for the latest, greatest Melendez facility…there were other stories—ones that put strong-arming landowners in the lightweight category.

Machine Melendez was a monster company with a history of monstrous deeds to account for its greatness. It was the brainchild of Mexican immigrant Danilo Melendez. The parts and services giant had boasted profits in the billions for the past fifteen years and multimillion-dollar balance sheets during the twenty-five prior years.

Even with the economic downturn, Machine Melendez managed to come out smelling distinctly rose-like. Danilo Melendez was a savvy businessman who saw the benefit in a diverse industry. Machine Melendez was not only a parts-and-services dynamo. There were holdings in the hospitality, finance and medical industries.

For all the accolades, however, rumors of corruption remained. Such were often the grumblings of jealous competitors. There were occasions still where many seemed to hold merit.

One of the more outrageous claimed Danilo Melendez had ties to a drug cartel out of Mexico City and that he'd served as a money launderer for the organization. It had been stated that in addition to the monetary benefit, Dan's laundering efforts were repaid in cheap labor from undocumented workers.

None of it could be proven, of course. No one rode the waves of the American dream the way Melendez had without covering any misdeeds with a host of admirable efforts…and friends.

Danilo Melendez boasted as many high-powered connections as he did business deals. Whatever negative attention the man may have attracted from the authorities, it wasn't enough to have any formal investigations launched.

Dan's friends were everywhere. Even in the most humble of communities. The man was well-known for sharing his very considerable wealth. Charity galas, hefty donations to public housing beautification and security efforts, child care initiatives—Machine Melendez was well loved by the people.

That was where Setha came in. Whatever her father's true reputation, she was proud of the charitable efforts of the company and her job to promote them. The head of Melendez Corporate Charities, she took her responsibilities seriously but let her staff receive the accolades and act as the face of the organization. She had no problems taking a backseat. Her image wasn't important. After all, in the Melendez family, if one was despised, they all were.

Spite was certainly what Avra Ross had to feel for Samson, Setha mused while scanning the purely sexist ads again. She wondered if Khouri Ross had seen them and what *his* impressions were. Though they'd never met, his reputation had preceded him.

He was the only son of a respected publisher. She knew Basil Ross made few moves without consulting his right hand. Word had it Khouri Ross was exceptionally good at everything he did.

Setha browsed the glossy shots and wondered whether he was truly a *cooler* head or one of the alpha male varieties she knew so well.

"What the hell are you doin'?" Khouri caught his sister's arm and tugged her back from the door just as her hand folded over the lever. "You can't just go bustin' in on the man like that."

"Well, what's the problem?" Avra propped fists to her slender hips and frowned. "Obviously somethin's up with him."

"And it's probably somethin' he doesn't want to discuss with his kids."

Avra blinked. "You think it's about a woman?"

"Jesus, Av." Khouri grimaced over her bewilderment. "Some folks do mix a little pleasure into their lives from time to time, you know? The man deserves that, doesn't he?"

Avra waited a beat and then nodded. "Yeah…yeah he does." Their mother had died over a decade earlier and, by all accounts, Basil hadn't looked at another woman since.

"Anyway, I don't think this is about a woman." Khouri's gaze was fixed on his father's office door then.

The admission fueled Avra's determination again. "Well, let's go find out what's goin' on."

"Wait, Av, that's not the way."

His hushed words stopped her easily. The tone never failed to deter Avra from whatever course of action she'd chosen. No one could argue that Khouri Ross had a sixth sense for selecting the right course of action. His batting average was so impressive in that regard that few saw the benefit of making a move until Khouri voiced his opinion. Avra simply slapped her hands to her sides and waited.

Doris Shipman was returning to her office then. "Hey, darlins!" she called.

Khouri slanted his sister a wink. "Hey, Miss Doris, you're just all over the place this mornin'."

"Honey, you said it!" Doris waved one hand above her head. "I'm startin' to feel like a chicken with my head cut off."

"Well, you're by far the prettiest chicken I've ever seen."

Doris waved her hand again, giggling like a high school girl instead of a great-grandmother. "Don't you even start that flattery, Khouri. I'm too busy to be swoonin' over compliments today."

Khouri didn't let up and Doris clearly didn't mind all that much. Avra leaned against the doorway of Doris's office and observed the scene. She pitied the woman who tried to ignore her brother. It'd be interesting to bet on how long one could resist should he put the full force of his charm to work then.

"We're sorry to be barging in on you here, Miss Doris, when you're so busy," Khouri was saying once talk of the new grandbaby and the fishing trip Mr. Shipman took to Lake Jackson had ended. "We just wanted to check in on Dad. After the way he raced out of the meeting…we thought there might be something we could help him with."

The expression dimmed on Doris's light honey-toned face, losing some of the illumination it held when talk had surrounded her family. "Oh, dear…" She fidgeted with her pearl necklace and glanced toward Basil's door. "It's not about business."

"Is he all right, Miss D?" Khouri moved closer to Doris, cupping her elbow lightly.

Again, Doris angled her head to check Basil's door. Satisfied by the level of privacy, she patted Khouri's chest. "He's gotten bad news about a friend, a colleague, almost like a brother really."

"No," Avra breathed, bolting from the doorway then. "Av!"

Avra was already walking into her father's office without so much as a knock to announce herself. Basil didn't seem bothered by the intrusion. He barely turned his head toward the door when it opened.

"Daddy?" Avra rushed around the desk, falling to her knees before Basil's chair. Her large, coffee-brown gaze searched his face almost half a minute. "Is it Mr. C, Daddy?" she asked, referring to her father's oldest friend, Wade Cornelius.

Basil nodded, cupping Avra's face when she gasped.

"Shh…" He gestured sweetly and pulled her close as her eyes pooled with water. "Shh…"

"What happened, Daddy?" Her voice was muffled in his shirt as they embraced.

"They…they say they found him dead."

Khouri stepped deeper into the large sunken office in the uppermost corner of the building.

"Found him?" Avra squeezed her father's shoulder. "How? When— Do they suspect—?"

"Shh, baby, shh… They don't know much more than that just yet." He kissed her forehead and patted the small of her back. "I need a little more time to myself, sugar, all right?"

"Let's go, Av," Khouri called before she thought about asking more questions. He moved behind the desk, gently but firmly pulling Avra from Basil's lap.

"It's okay, Av," he soothed while leading her to the door. Before leaving, Avra caught Khouri sending a narrowed meaningful look toward his father. Basil barely sent him a wave, before turning his chair to face the windows lining the rear wall of the room.

Avra was shaking noticeably by the time they were back out in the hall. Khouri's soft tone and reassuring rubs to her back had her measurably calm soon after.

"Mr. C?" he queried when he and Avra were seated in the small waiting area outside the office.

Avra studied her hands smothered in one of Khouri's and took solace in the comfort it instilled. "Wade Cornelius. He was my mentor here right out of college. He was a very respected writer—more than Pop even once they got the magazine up and running." She smiled. "Daddy was more interested in the business end of things—left the writing to Mr. C." Covering her face in her hands, she inhaled for a few seconds and then continued. "He was a wonderful man. I learned a lot from him." She sniffed. "That was back when I was naive enough to think I had what it took to be a hard-nosed journalist."

Khouri listened intently, cupping Avra's cheek when she wept. "You gonna be okay, honey?"

"Sorry." She sniffed again frowning at herself for losing reign over her emotions. "Didn't mean to get sappy."

"Stop," Khouri whispered, using his thumb to brush a tear from her cheek. "You're entitled. Can I do anything?"

Avra laughed amid her weeping. "Just don't tell me you can't take over the Melendez ad account. I'm definitely not in the mood to deal with that or anything else heavy right now," she said, watching as her little brother graced her with one of the adorably guileless smiles that made her heart melt even when she was mad enough to spit nails at him.

"No sweat," he said.

Avra brushed his face. "Go handle your business." She kept her smile in place until he was gone.

Setha had a full evening planned that night. It was to take place right there before the TV in her sitting room.

"What a lucky girl I am." She sighed, grimly eyeing the two hefty folders on the pine coffee table before her. She'd gone through the Melendez ad file several times, but would take another look once more for good measure before tomorrow morning's meeting.

The file that held her full attention just then was the one simply labeled with a question mark. Everything inside had proven to be one big riddle after another. Setha fingered the pink message slip that had started it all.

"What now?" she asked herself. Her "stalker" had effectively ruined the meeting she had hoped to have with Raquel Ross at her club. It was a good thing she hadn't alerted the woman beforehand, Setha thought. She wondered whether she should risk another meeting and then decided it could be a moot point after tomorrow.

The entire reason for visiting the club had been to get a sense of the Ross family—to discover what side of the fence they were really on.

Hmph. Setha leaned forward to brace her elbows to her knees. Would she even know how to make the distinction? Lately, it'd been very difficult for her to tell the good guys from the bad.

That thought made her think of her rescuer from the night in the alley. Definitely a good guy. She hadn't even told him "thank you" when she ran from his car....

She was lost in her thoughts until something caught her ear from the news broadcast on TV. Frowning, she moved aside the folds of the chiffon robe in search for the remote which rested beneath her rump on the sofa cushions.

"Come on…" she muttered, clicking the rewind button on the DVR.

"…was found dead in his condo. Police have not determined cause of death at this time. Wade Cornelius had a well-respected reputation for fair and intelligent reporting. He will be missed. Once again, Wade Cornelius, dead at…"

"Oh, my God," Setha breathed.

Chapter 3

"Are you sure it's all right?" Setha was asking the next morning when she stood in the executive hall of the *Ross Review*.

"It's just fine, honey," Marta Leonard drawled, already leading the way to her boss's office. "Khouri's just finishing up with another matter—he'll be along directly. Already asked that you be shown in here to wait 'til he gets back. Coffee, honey?"

"Oh, uh…no, no, thank you. I'm fine." Setha put down her things and smiled.

When Marta was gone, Setha regretted turning down the coffee but knew it was for the best. That indulgence would definitely be a mistake since her stomach was already a barrel of nerves.

Following the news broadcast on Wade Cornelius's death, she needed something different to focus on—to settle her mind. Reviewing more of the lurid shots for the proposed Melendez ads wasn't the ticket. Instead, she decided to do some research on her new business associate. As a result, her nerves rewound again quite nicely.

The second eldest and only son in a family of four kids, Khouri Ross had a reputation that could epitomize grace under fire. He was known for being wickedly intelligent, very soft-spoken. It was rumored that, when he walked into a meeting, folks waited for *his* input and tended to agree. Additionally, and probably the asset which fueled the power of the others, were the looks encasing the package.

And what a package. Setha recalled the pictures she'd uncovered. The man was definitely...to-die-for. Tall, he had the sort of lean powerful frame that made any piece of clothing look good. Deep-set eyes, she couldn't make out the color only that they were bright and striking. Then there was the strong jaw and cleft chin... She wondered if the pictures did him justice?

She'd lived among gorgeous men all her life. It went without saying that she was well aware how difficult they could be if they were vain enough. If Khouri Ross gave her half the grief her brothers were capable of, this business association would be yet another level of hell in her once quiet and easy life.

Shaking off what she could of her nervousness, Setha began a stroll of the office. Smoothing clammy hands across the seat of her putty-colored low-rise skirt, she more closely observed her surroundings. Sadly, the stroll did little to settle her nerves.

On top of to-die-for handsome, intelligent and respected, she could also add "accomplished" to the list. The mahogany shelving which lined the walls abounded with plaques, trophies and pictures of Khouri Ross accepting awards…and looking very nice while he did it.

What really caught her eyes though were the magazine covers. How had this man escaped her radar? *Because you're a party-dodging workaholic who'll trust a man to friendship but nothing more.*

Setha blinked. "Shut up," she told the silent, responding voice. Stepping closer to the center shelf, she took a closer look at one of the magazine covers. In actuality, it was a calendar cover. Some sort of eligible bachelor thing for one of the city's numerous big-name charities. She only recognized it because two of her brothers were in it. Setha was more interested in scanning Khouri Ross's page.

Obviously the calendar had little to do with assisting one in finding the day's date. Setha's full mouth curved into a knowing smile, observing the sexy beefcakes inside—her brothers excluded. She gave a playful grimace at their photos and flipped to August and Khouri's shot.

Every entry was created as a centerfold and Setha took great pleasure in extending the sheet to its full length. She was letting out a low whistle in reference to the devastating image before her eyes, when the life-size version walked through the door.

Khouri softly cleared his throat.

The low rumbling did the trick.

The calendar fell from suddenly weak fingers when Setha spotted the man twenty feet across the room. Her charcoal-black stare widened in tandem to her mouth forming a larger O.

"Sorry." She blinked, stopping to collect the calendar and put it back in its place.

"Damn," she whispered when it fell and she stopped again to grab it. Expelling a slow breath, she set it back on the shelf a bit more deliberately.

Khouri watched, smiling more broadly after her curse. She stood and was walking toward him with her hand outstretched when he began to frown.

"Nice to meet you, Mr. Ross." Setha was offering her hand while introducing herself. The frown he wore was hard to miss.

"I'm sorry." She glanced awkwardly across her shoulder. "I didn't mean to go through your things."

Slowly, *very* slowly, Khouri shook himself out of his stupor. "No, it—it's all right." He took the hand she offered.

"Thank you—" she let out the breath she didn't realize she was holding "—for, um, taking the meeting." *Dammit, Seth, get a hold of yourself!* When he just stood there staring, she swallowed and wondered whether he'd mind her doing the same. His pictures didn't do him justice. No sirree, they didn't do him justice at all.

Taking Setha Melendez's lead, Khouri swallowed as well and with no small effort. He even managed a slight nod, while waving toward the office living area. "Would you like to sit?"

Nodding, Setha flexed her hand a bit once he'd released it from his firm grip. She was taking her place in one of the deep merlot-colored armchairs before the desk when she noticed he'd moved to the living area and was waiting for her to join him there. She batted at a loose wavy tendril that had slipped from her coiffure and collected her things before meeting him across the room. He was standing near a long black sofa, so she took that as her cue to sit there.

Remember to blink, she told herself, praying he'd start first. Her mind was too busy making mental images of him to formulate words.

"Looks like we've got some work ahead of us."

"Yes." She practically breathed the word in response to his observation. She blinked again, reminding herself that she didn't want the man to think she was a total idiot. Putting her mind to the task at hand, she reached over to grab the folder she'd been reviewing over the last several days.

"Looks like your sister and my brother got a lot of work done."

"And didn't come up with much."

She seasoned her shrug with a smirk. "I can tell they put a lot of effort into it."

Khouri's shoulder barely rose beneath the walnut-brown shirt and matching suit coat he wore. "A lot of effort may've gone in but a lot of crap came out."

Setha raised a brow while observing the glossy photo she held. "You don't agree that sex sells?"

He only spared a second's glance at the photo before his uncommon hazel eyes returned to her face. "Only if it's good sex," he said.

The glossy fell from Setha's fingers that had once again gone weak.

Khouri bent to retrieve it. Setha fought the urge to shift in her spot as his bright gaze made an astute trek along the length of her legs below the uneven hemline of her skirt.

"So how should we begin this?" she asked once he'd straightened.

Khouri passed her the photo. "That file you're holding?" he prompted and waited for her nod. He cocked his head toward his desk. "Start by tossin' it in the wastebasket."

Setha threw back her head and laughed. Loudly.

"Does your sister know how much you hate her work?" Setha relaxed a bit more on the sofa.

Khouri leaned back, crossing his legs at the ankles. "She hates it herself, so no harm done."

"Right." Setha scanned the photo again. "So is it my brother's take on it that you hate?"

"Not at all." He was already shaking his head. "It's just obvious that he's going against what he really wants and tryin' to please Avra at the same time. That was his first mistake."

A tiny frown worked its way between Setha's long, arched brows. "What is it you think he really wants?"

Khouri motioned toward the photo. "May I?" Taking the artwork, he used two other glossies to crop the photo in question.

Setha watched with bland interest. "A woman in a bikini standing over a caption that reads 'Buy Melendez.'" She smirked. "You're serious?"

Khouri regarded her more intently. "Machine Melendez is a male-dominated company selling a male-dominated product."

Setha's laughter was a bit less humor filled then. "Women *do* buy the occasional alternator, Mr. Ross."

"Khouri."

Dammit, she thought, did he have to make her want to moan when she was trying to make a valid point?

"Can I get you anything?" he offered, easily noticing her strained expression.

Setha only shook her head to decline.

"Your point's well taken," Khouri continued, "and in Samson's defense, what makes him so good at promoting Melendez is that he speaks to the majority of his clientele and he speaks in their language."

"Chauvinism. Sexism."

"Good guesses." Khouri grinned when she gave him a playful wave. "It is what it is. But if Melendez wants advertising in the *Review* we're gonna have to come up with something that speaks to all Melendez clientele."

"Equally?" Setha's tone was hopeful.

Khouri pushed aside the photos. "We're not miracle workers, Ms. Melendez."

"Setha, please."

"Setha."

A shiver kissed her skin beneath the material of her white French-cuffed shirt. Thinning her lips, she steeled herself against reacting to it. "So do you know what your sister wants for this campaign?"

"That's easy." Khouri took the photos and turned them facedown. "Nothing. She doesn't think we should even be doing business with your family's company."

Once again that morning, Setha broke into full-bodied laughter.

Avra set the lock on her office door and then took a seat on the edge of her desk. Facing her view of downtown Houston, she dialed out and waited for the connection.

"Avra!" a cheerful feminine voice greeted.

"Off the record, Gwen."

"Heffa," Gwen Bennett huffed in the most affectionate tone. "So what's up?"

Avra trailed fingers through the short, glossy, onyx-colored curls covering her head. "Did you hear about Wade Cornelius?"

"Yeah…" Gwen's sigh came through the line. "The man was a legend. I'm pretty sure the *Houston Journal*'s got some sort of memorial planned for him in the op-ed section later in the week."

"And that's all?"

"Well, that's what—"

Avra rolled her eyes. She could practically see the veteran reporter's internal antennae going up.

"What's up, Av?"

"You knew he was my mentor, Gwen."

"Yeah…" Gwen sighed again, that time realizing how hard the man's death must have hit her friend. "I'm sorry if I sounded crass, I—"

"Have you heard anything else about his death?" Avra moved off her desk and closer to the windows. "All it said on the news was that he'd been—been found… Do you know whether the authorities suspect some foul play?"

"Honestly, Av, I haven't heard a thing. Is this…something you want me to dig around in?"

Avra hedged instead of offering a prompt reply.

"I promise not to print anything without talking to you first. But, Av, if it turns out that foul play *did* account for the death, you know it'll be news."

"I know." Avra turned her back on the view and worried the hemline of her silver ruffled blouse. "Look, just do whatever you can to find out whatever you can and keep it quiet for as long as you can, all right?"

"Avra…honey, don't take this wrong but do you think I *will* find something?"

Avra began to wear a path before the floor-to-ceiling windows in the office. "I can't say one way or another. I mean, Mr. C was no spring chicken—high blood pressure, diabetes…so who knows? But it's nagging at me. Whether anything's up or not, the cops'll hide it for as long as they can, and I'm not patient enough to wait on them to share the news."

"Understood. All right then, girl. I'll be in touch."

The call ended and Avra cradled her forehead in her palm.

After a lengthy discussion, Setha and Khouri broke for a brainstorming session. Seated on opposite sides of the office, they scribbled ideas for possible Machine Melendez ads.

At least, Setha scribbled. Khouri stared. It was all he could do to get through the first hour of their discussion that morning. It would have probably been a chore for him to keep his full attention on business anyway.

It went without saying that Setha Melendez was a beauty. It was no surprise that she was tall coming from a family of giants—same as him, Khouri thought. What was a surprise was the sweet, husky voice that cracked every now and then in the most adorable way. Unlike her brothers who'd inherited their complexion from their father, Setha's skin was a flawless dark chocolate, courtesy of her mother.

Then, there was everything else. Her curves. The blue-black waves of hair bound in the tight glossy ball atop her head. Then there were the midnight-colored eyes that could drown a man and the mouth that promised heaven.

While the physical surprises abounded and delighted, they didn't take his mind off the fact that she'd sought refuge in his car just two nights prior. Of all the mysteries he intended to solve about her, that was the one he most wanted answers to.

"Lunch?" he proposed when she looked up to find him watching her.

"Oh...thank you, but no." She scooted to the edge of the sofa. "I'm supposed to have a late lunch with my staff."

"Well, then." Khouri left his place behind the desk and went to meet her in the center of the room. "Guess we'll have lots to talk about." He smiled toward the pad she'd been scribbling on.

She eased it into her tote and nodded. "I'll clear time with my staff so we can schedule meetings and put this thing to bed." She coughed, the phrase having left her mouth before her brain could process it.

Khouri held his laughter, knowing he'd only embarrass her more than she already was. "May I take you to your car?" he asked, bringing his hand to the small of her back but not touching her there.

Setha raised a hand, shaking her head as she did so. "I've already taken up enough of your time."

"Hold on." He went back to his desk, leaning across it and grabbing the phone. "Hey," he greeted softly when Marta answered. "Call down to security and tell them to have somebody down there to show Ms. Melendez to her car."

"I appreciate that," Setha said when he rejoined her in the middle of the room. "But I can get myself to the car just fine."

"I know that, but this is for Sam's benefit." Khouri's sleek brows rose in acknowledgment of her curiosity.

"I'm sure he didn't much like sending his baby sister into the lion's den. Having sisters myself, I know I wouldn't care for it much, either." Bright eyes scanned her body quickly yet intensely. "Least I can do is have security give you an escort."

"Well, thank you." She almost whispered the words.

"You're welcome. I'll call you." His voice was just as soft.

Setha walked out less than half a minute later and Khouri ordered himself to stop at his office door—not to follow her down the hall. He watched even after she had disappeared into one of the elevators.

"Put your tongue back in your mouth, baby," Marta said when she walked past.

Khouri rolled his eyes and returned to his office. Marta's laughter followed.

Chapter 4

Marta was handling a call when Avra dropped by her brother's office. She pointed to the door to silently inquire if he was in.

Covering the phone's mouthpiece, Marta's eyes shifted quickly toward the door. "Yeah, but in a weird mood."

"And this is news?"

"He's been acting funny since Ms. Melendez left around lunch."

"Ah…" Avra's expression turned smug. "I told him he'd be floored."

"*Floored* ain't the half of it."

"Thanks, Mart," Avra said, letting the woman get back to her phone call.

She applied a fast knock to the door and stepped into the office calling Khouri's name. He was behind his desk, somberly swiveling his chair to and fro. Avra had to call his name three times before catching his attention.

She whistled when he pulled his fist from his chin and looked over at her. "Damn! Floored *ain't* the half of it. You looked downright steamrolled, baby brother."

Khouri smiled but made no effort to provide a verbal confirmation…or denial.

"Come on, out with it." Avra moved aside folders from a corner of the desk and planted her butt in the space. "So? How'd it go?"

"Not now, Av."

"Uh-uh, I've been waiting all day for you to tell me about it."

"Later."

"Well what? Do I need to be concerned?" She wasn't put off by the black look he sent her.

"I mean, if I need to be concerned—tell me." She folded her arms across the front of the ruffled blouse and feigned exasperation. "It *is* my name on the account. I should know if it's about to take a swan dive down the toilet."

"Bullshit." Khouri worked the bridge of his nose between his thumb and forefinger. "But all right."

"What?"

"It's got nothin' to do with the ads. You just want to know what happened with her."

"Khouri…" That time, Avra feigned innocence. "That's not even true. I need this idea of Dad's to work. I'm absolutely *not* trying to have to deal with Samson Melendez again. Ever."

Khouri didn't have to look Avra's way to detect the disappointment on her part. Was she aware of it? he wondered.

"So. About the meeting?"

"Jesus, Avra." Khouri left his desk then said, "She's incredible, all right?"

Avra leaned over his desk, bracing her weight on one elbow. "Trophy material, huh?"

"Ha!" He laughed over the phrasing, but nodded. "And then some, but more than that—a lot more."

"Wow." Avra couldn't pull her eyes away from her brother's face. He looked positively thunderstruck. "I still can't believe you've never met her—seen her. I would've expected you to have scoped that piece of eye candy a long time ago."

"Yeah…" Khouri's thunderstruck look showed traces of unease. "Well I *thought* I'd never met her," he said and rubbed the back of his neck while walking the perimeter of his office.

Avra's long stare widened in anticipation of Khouri sharing a bit of sexy dirt.

"Forget it," he flatly refused, easily reading her expression. "Maybe *met* is too strong of a word."

Avra hung her head and shook it. "Now I'm completely confused." She was, however, sitting up moments later once Khouri explained how and where he'd originally *met* Setha Melendez in the alley behind Raquel's club.

Overwhelmed, Avra could only sit with her mouth open in amazement. "All right…is it possible for you to go over this once more and slowly—I mean like funeral-procession slowly?"

He grinned. "Story ain't gonna change, darlin'."

"But what's it all about? What'd she say when you asked her?"

"I didn't ask her."

"Well, dammit, Khouri. Why not?"

"Hell, Avra!" Khouri lost the tether he kept on what had the potential to be a considerable temper. "I wasn't about to ask her somethin' like that."

"Why not?"

"I just met her, for Christ's sakes!"

"Well, what do *you* think it's about?" Avra asked after waiting a beat.

A low sound, definitely in the neighborhood of a growl, churned deep in Khouri's throat. The familiar pressure tightened his palms as he thought of the night. "A man chases a woman down an alley and she prefers hiding in my car to going inside a club full of people. She didn't even wait around for me to call for help." He pushed both hands into his pockets. "I'm thinkin' she knew the jackass."

"But that doesn't make sense. I mean, what man in his right mind would chase Setha Melendez down an alley if he *knew* it was Setha Melendez and who her family was? And that she's got three brothers built like tanks?"

Khouri shrugged. "So what are *you* thinking?"

"I'm thinkin' you should ask her what the hell is up. You had her take refuge in your car, for crap's sake— she at least owes you an explanation."

"Right." Khouri stroked the light shadow of a beard covering otherwise flawless caramel-toned skin and he let his frustration show. "So tell me how you'd feel if you'd just met Sam Melendez and he came questioning *you* about something like that?"

"Why—" Avra closed her mouth, and then opened it again. "Why do you always have to make everything about me and Samson Melendez?"

"Just tryin' to put it in a perspective you can relate to."

"Fine." Avra raised a hand in weariness. "I can see my input isn't needed or desired."

Khouri gave her a mock salute. "You're a quick study, Av."

Avra gave her brother the finger and then waltzed out of his office without further discussion.

Alone then, Khouri admitted the valid point his sister had raised. It didn't make sense that a man would run down Setha Melendez in an alley especially if he knew who she was. He'd have to know he was a dead man if her family found him.

Khouri sat on the desk corner Avra had vacated. He was sure few men could handle losing a woman like the beautiful Ms. Melendez.... If the incident he'd witnessed was in fact a lover's spat gone bad in the worst way, had it jaded her enough to swear off all men?

Whoa, man. He went to slosh a little bourbon into a glass at the wall bar in his office.

His sister, whether she knew it or not, was already gaga over one Melendez. There was no sense in him jumping into the same pot. Of course that, in no way, meant that he couldn't do everything in his power to find out what ran her into his car that night and why.

Setha was searching her phone for a number, when she spotted Samson reclining behind her desk while he chatted with her assistant, Valerie Lennin. She cleared her throat noisily to cut through the sound of Valerie's high-pitched giggles. "Something you forgot to ask me during lunch, Val?" she asked once the room had gone silent.

Recognizing her boss's sarcasm, Valerie offered a tight smile. "I'll just be at my desk." Twirling a dark blond lock around her finger, she put her most flirtatious smile in place. "Bye, Samson."

"What?" Setha greeted her brother when they were left alone.

"Just stopped by to find out how the meeting went." Sam stroked his jaw and regarded her with cool intent lacing his dark stare. "Did Avra keep buttin' in to your meeting? Bet she didn't let you get a word in."

Tossing her things to a chair before the desk, Setha grinned. "Actually, she didn't butt in once—never saw her while I was there."

"Is that right?"

Setha took great pleasure in the sound of his voice. She left off grinning though. "I'll be back over there soon if there's…some message you want me to deliver—"

"You can tell her to go screw herself." Sam left the desk chair tugging on the gray-and-black suspenders that complemented his shirt.

"Go screw—*herself?*" Setha pretended to be confused and rested her palm to her cheek. "Isn't that something *you'd* want to take part in?" She let loose her laughter at the look he gave.

"This is serious business, Set."

"We know that, Sam. Khouri and I will give this our best efforts."

"How's it lookin' so far?"

Setha gave an exaggerated sigh and brought her hands to her hips. "We're gonna have to make some changes, Sam."

"What kind of changes?"

"Big ones."

"Well, what—all right, all right." He raised his hands at her look and reconsidered his next question. "So are you comin' over to Pop's for dinner this weekend?"

"I'll try, but I've got so much work." Setha latched onto the excuse she'd used for the past several weeks. "With this Melendez/Ross account campaign everything's been busier. Like you said, 'This is serious,'" she noted when his stare progressively hardened. "It's gonna take a lot for me to stay on top of it."

"You haven't been over for dinner in weeks. Everybody's noticed."

"When?" Setha's husky voice cracked as laughter intervened. "Between all of your dates and Daddy's golfing weekends?" She rolled her eyes and went behind her desk. "Don't act like all of you sit around the dinner table every Sunday missing me."

"All right. We don't, but we damn well know somethin' ain't right with you."

"Sam—"

"Hush," he said, index finger slicing the air. "I won't stand for it, Set. None of us will. Now you can either come clean with us or we can have fun makin' a big ole mess while we find out on our own." He reached across the desk and grabbed her hand to tug her into the kiss he placed on her forehead. "See you soon," he called on his way out of the door.

Setha turned and propped her rump on the edge of the desk. The very last thing she needed was Samson, Paolo and Lugo Melendez making a "big ole mess." On the other hand, she couldn't argue the point that having them make a mess might keep her dangerous pursuer off her back long enough to find out if the guy was just some weird stalker she'd attracted or if her entire family had something to fear.

She'd hoped to have more time to scope out the *Ross Review* but hadn't once thought of doing that after meeting Khouri Ross. If first impressions were anything to go on, the Rosses were quite deserving of all the respect they wielded in and around Houston.

What she'd uncovered so far, though, told her there was definitely some connection between her "stalker" and Wade Cornelius. Now the man was dead.... She had to find out more regarding that connection. So far it was her only lead and it'd been sheer dumb luck that had brought her to it. Digging deeper would probably bring her more of nothing, but she had to check it out at least.

It would help to have someone to bounce her suspicions off of, she couldn't deny that. A confidant, however, would either help solve this thing, or think she was crazy and involve her family. If they weren't involved already.

"Sorry I missed you earlier, Gwen."

Gwen Bennett was on her way out of the conference room following the *Houston Journal*'s weekly interdepartmental meeting.

"'Salright, Brew, wasn't anything that couldn't wait," she told her colleague.

Brewster Keegan's expression personified confidence. "Finally takin' me up on my dinner invitation, huh?"

Gwen shook her head, chuckling softly while she did so. "Brew, you know I don't date men with girlfriends—even if girlfriend knows she's not the only one."

"You drive a hard bargain, G." Brewster didn't appear offended or discouraged. "So I guess that means you came by my office to talk business, huh?"

"Got it." Gwen gave a toss of her chin-length bob and held her portfolio in front of her chest. "I wanted to talk to you about something you said a few weeks back—about Wade Cornelius."

"Yeah, my story on the murders."

"Murders?"

"The immigrant murders, you know?" He nudged her arm as if to jog her memory. "Cops have squat, but they know all the vics worked for some part of Machine Melendez."

"So what's that got to do with Wade Cornelius?"

Brewster moved in closer. "The connection between the victims and Melendez is big news and Ross hasn't released it yet."

"So? Neither has the *Journal.*"

A sobering light filtered Brewster's dark blue gaze then. "You and Avra Ross are pretty good pals, right?"

Gwen rolled her eyes toward the sienna-colored pumps she wore. "That hurts, Brew."

"I'm sorry, G. I didn't mean for it to." He nudged her elbow again before glancing back across his shoulder. "It's just we're not tryin' to rock the boat releasin' this stuff. 'Specially when we suspect a cover-up."

"And you suspect Ross?"

"We don't, but all the vics are MM employees. Ever since Cornelius wrote that first story back in the day on the company, Melendez has been made to look like some kind of white knight when everyone knows they're not."

Gwen tapped her fingers to her chin, absorbing the information.

Brewster brought his hand to her elbow again but held on that time. "I wouldn't mind sharing the spotlight with you if you can use your connections with the lovely Ms. Ross to find out if holding back the info was intentional on the *Review*'s end."

"I wouldn't expect her to tell me all that, Brew. We're *pals* but still competitors, remember?"

Brewster slipped a hand into a pocket on his green trousers. "We're bankin' on the fact that Ross isn't tryin' to run a story there. They've always seemed to be intent on protecting the Machine's image. On *this* side of town, we're workin' to pull back that image and show the true face of Melendez. I swear we're not out to take down a colleague in the process."

"Basil Ross and Dan Melendez have been friends a long time. There has to be a reason why he'd cover them that way. Maybe they're trying to get to the bottom of all this, too."

"I hope so." Brewster shrugged. "Because otherwise it means they're in it with 'em."

Gwen tilted her head. "In what?"

Brewster looked grim. "In whatever all this is about."

"He's out of control, dammit! Wade Cornelius wasn't to be touched."

"He thinks they're all to blame in this. In a way, he's right."

Static crackled on the phone line for several moments.

"He's right, but killing Cornelius has pushed this thing forward too fast. His death might get too many smart folks digging and making links we don't need made just yet. Put a leash on him."

Chapter 5

Setha muttered a curse when her fourth flush produced the same dismal results. She used one yellow work-gloved hand to push back a tuft of hair that had fallen from the ratty ponytail she wore.

"Thank you, Jesus…" She sighed when the doorbell caught her ear. She kicked the toilet bowl with the toe of a black hiking boot and stomped from the guest bathroom to the front door.

"My day just keeps getting better," she grumbled after opening the door to find Khouri Ross on her porch. It was just her luck the man would have to pay a visit while catching her in khaki cutoffs and a tight T-shirt after trying to fix the toilet.

"This a bad time?" he was polite enough to ask while smirking toward the plunger she carried.

"I thought you were the plumber." She managed a miserable smile.

Khouri cocked a brow and tugged at his earlobe. "I never heard that one before." He made a pretense at turning away. "Should I go?"

"Oh, no, no, don't leave." She extended her free hand and then caught herself, pressing her lips together. "Please come in." She added a flourishing wave. "I'm praying the plumber can help since my efforts aren't doing the trick." She shook the plunger.

"May I help?"

"No." Her voice held a chuckle. "I wouldn't dream of it. You're my guest."

"I wouldn't have offered if I minded."

"Trust me, it's fine." She pushed back another tuft of hair. "And my day's goin' badly enough without having a houseguest unclog my toilet."

Her words stoked the serious side of his attention. Soon, he was dwarfing her leggy frame with his taller one.

"What's wrong?"

Setha hesitated. For an instant, she believed if she told him the problem, everything would be better. A second later her voice of reason was telling her to stop being stupid and she blinked herself out from under the spell he cast.

"Just one of those days." She drew the back of one hand across her nose and led the way into the living room. "Can I get you anything?" She remembered the plunger and shrugged. "Maybe you should help yourself. You're free to have anything."

"Really?" He kept his distance, but his light gaze spoke volumes.

Setha ignored her heart throbbing in her throat. "Bar's

over there. Kitchen's down that hall to the right." She looked toward the plunger again. "I better put this up."

Alone in the living room, Khouri eased his hands into his jean pockets and observed his surroundings. He enjoyed the cozy brightness of the lower levels in the spacious River Oaks home. For a time, he stood somewhat captivated by the view of the elegant courtyard shaded with vibrant brush and trees. The house certainly mimicked its owner, Khouri thought. There was just a hint of something reserved yet bright and open. At least that's what he felt when he was around her. Having the chance to prove that was a possibility that was beginning to affect his sleep.

"Sorry 'bout that," Setha called, wiping her hands to the seat of her shorts when she returned to the room.

At the bar, Khouri took it upon himself to fix her a drink while he prepared one for himself.

"Bottoms up," he said when it appeared she'd just cradle the glass in her hand.

He took her arm and Setha gladly drank down some of the liquid to calm herself as they walked toward the sofa.

"This is some house," Khouri complimented after they'd enjoyed their drinks in easy silence. "You lived here long?"

"All my life." Setha smiled wistfully. "It's where I grew up."

Looking up at the vaulted ceilings, Khouri nodded while recalling that her father lived in the city.

"I took it over when Daddy moved."

"You like being so isolated?" Khouri sat then set his elbows to his knees while making the sly inquiry.

Setha sipped more of her drink and shrugged. "I

know this place like the back of my hand. I could never be afraid here." Milliseconds after the declaration, she shivered as memories of a rather frightful evening came to mind. She drank more of the bourbon.

Leaning back on the sofa, Khouri studied her reaction.

She could feel his eyes on her and, while it wasn't a bad feeling, she couldn't take a chance on him seeing more than she wanted to reveal. Somehow, she believed that wouldn't be hard for him to do.

Setting the empty glass on an end table, she forced brightness into her expression. "So tell me about your name—pretty uncommon."

"Strange, you mean."

"No." She smiled at the way he flatly accepted what he perceived as fact. "Not at all... Is there a meaning?"

Khouri's smile came through. "It's Arabic for 'priest.' My mother read it somewhere, fell in love with it...."

Riveted by the explanation, Setha had curled her legs beneath her on the sofa as she listened. "Have you ever had any aspirations?" she asked when he quieted.

Khouri studied the beaded glass he held. "I wondered whether my mother wanted something like that for me. I toyed with the idea when she passed."

"I'm sorry." Setha pressed her lips together and resisted the urge to reach out to him.

"Thanks." He massaged his jaw briefly and sat up straight on the sofa. "I'm sorry for your loss, as well. How long since your own mother passed?"

"I was in middle school." Her voice went softer. "My brothers helped my dad raise me."

Khouri's hazel stare reflected a hint of knowing. "Protective, huh?"

Setha laughed, full and easy. "*That's* an understatement."

"Guess bringing a date home to meet the family ain't an easy thing to do?"

Setha laughed more. "Men don't last long once my father and brothers find out about them."

"No one's good enough."

She considered her answer. "They figure if a guy isn't strong enough to stand up to them physically or mentally, then he's not strong enough to protect me or do right by me—in their opinion."

"And how do *you* feel about that?" Khouri watched the bridge he made with his fingers.

"I work too hard to worry about it. Anyway—" she sighed "—it's not so bad. I'm able to remain friends with the men I date."

Khouri smirked. "You must have lots of male friends."

"Tons."

Gaze trained on his hands, Khouri silently admitted that he wasn't sure how he felt about her answer.

"After meeting so many good guys—more interested in pleasing my family than me—I've decided to keep the men I meet on the friendship list and leave 'em there."

Khouri decided he liked those words much more. "Any of them promising enough to be taken off the list?" he asked anyway.

"And move into my bed, you mean?"

The pointed question had Khouri laughing and coughing. "More or less," he managed to say.

"Not yet." Setha studied him thoughtfully, and then nodded toward his glass when he looked her way. "Freshen your drink?"

Khouri passed his glass and watched her go to the bar.

"What kind of story?" Avra was asking Gwen Bennett when they spoke by phone later that afternoon. She listened to her friend explain that it'd be about Machine Melendez.

"Well, what's that got to do with—"

"One of my colleagues is asking questions about why *Ross Review* hasn't published a negative story about Melendez since Wade Cornelius's article about that suicide. Some guy who worked for Machine Melendez killed himself, remember?"

In her den, Avra lost what strength remained in her legs. Slowly, she settled down to the edge of a coffee table. "John Holloway," she said.

"Right. Anyway, there's the lack of negative press from *Ross* and the immigrant murders that haven't been discussed in the *Review,* either."

"Does the *Journal* think Melendez is somehow connected to 'em?"

Gwen hesitated.

"Don't bother. I guess sharing time's over."

"We aren't out to embarrass *Ross Review,* Av. But there *have* been questions about why you guys haven't made a peep about those victims being Melendez employees. If there's a cover-up going on here, Ross *could* be affected."

Gwen sighed. "I'm sorry, Av. I know you weren't expecting anything like this when you asked me to dig."

"Don't be stupid. I'm glad I asked. Listen, um—" Avra moved from the table "—we'll talk soon, all right?"

"Okay, girl. Have a good one."

"You, too." Avra wasted no time dialing out again seconds after the connection broke with Gwen. Paul Tristam's voice came through the line soon after.

"Hey, get in touch with David Crus and Noah Eames before you head home," she told her assistant, "and tell them I want to see 'em in my office tomorrow morning."

Khouri and Setha opened their electronic planners on their phones and set up meeting times for the next month. They hoped to have the campaign revisions complete long before then, but silently acknowledged how much they enjoyed each other's company.

Once the meetings were in place, Setha offered a tour of her home. Khouri wasn't about to refuse it. The tour ended with Setha showing off the courtyard Khouri had admired earlier.

"Next time I'll show you the firing range," she blurted out and then winced over being presumptuous.

"I can't wait." Khouri's translucent gaze harbored amusement as he watched her reaction. "You've got me curious."

"Oh? Never seen a firing range?"

"Funny." He rolled his eyes toward the manmade pond in the distance. "Actually I'm wondering whether you get any use out of it or if it's strictly for Sam, Pow and Lou," he said, referencing her brothers.

"Funny," Setha threw back. "I'll have you know that I get more use out of it than anyone." She sized him up.

"If you don't believe me, next time we can take out the rifles and I'll prove it."

Khouri didn't mind her seeing the intensity of his stare. "You're on," he said.

Their walk had taken them to the doors leading back into the living room. Setha was about to pull them open when Khouri dropped a hand over hers. Her eyes widened just slightly when he moved closer, towering over her again.

"I think you'll turn me down again if I ask you to have dinner with me." He studied the emblem on her T-shirt. "Am I right?" He looked up and focused then on pulling a tuft of hair from its clinging hold around the cuff of her ear.

Setha's hand weakened on the door lever as he rubbed her hair between his fingers. More than anything, she wanted to accept. Going out anywhere, except to work, had become as nerve-racking as trying to figure out why someone may have wanted her dead.

"I..." She closed her eyes briefly and sighed. "The plumber—he should'vc been here by now. He's supposed to call my cell when he's on his way—hopefully that'll be soon. I, um—I shouldn't risk missing him."

Khouri nodded his understanding. "Would I be overstepping if I asked again?"

Her smile was faint. "How could you be overstepping?"

"We're supposed to be about business."

"We can have dinner and still be about business."

He shook his head while dragging his gaze along her body. "Business would be the last thing I'd be about during dinner."

Setha commanded her lashes to remain still when

he moved even closer. The subtle ring of her mobile interrupted whatever may've happened. She fumbled for it and answered following a second's hesitation. It was the plumber letting her know he was approaching the road leading to her home. She ended the call and told Khouri who it was.

"Well, then." He moved to his full height.

Setha bit her lip while cursing the timing. Suddenly, Khouri dipped close again and she swallowed, praying he'd decided to kiss her. But he was only moving in to open the door.

"Any security on these doors?" he asked as they made their way into the living room.

"The best." Setha eased one hand into a side pocket on her shorts. "And I locked up before we took our walk. I used my phone to unsecure this lock when we were halfway through the courtyard."

"This electronic system is all you have?"

She nodded fast.

"No dogs? Guards?"

"I don't need all that!" She laughed.

"Don't you think you need somebody out at that gate you don't use?

"God, Khouri, you're worse than my brothers." She brought her other hand to her hip. "If it makes you feel better to know this, at night I buzz everyone in. No one gets through until I see who's on-screen."

"Why not use it round-the-clock?" he challenged, shutting the door and securing the lock. "If somebody wanted you bad enough, they could get through to you."

"If I didn't know better, I'd think you were trying to scare me on purpose."

"Hell." Khouri hung his head, massaging the side of his neck. "I'm sorry."

She shrugged. "'Sokay." She couldn't have been truly angry with him even if she tried. "You've got three sisters. My guess is being overly concerned comes naturally to you."

Khouri grinned. "You have no idea." He pressed a hand to his chest. "I really am sorry. The last thing I want to do is make you nervous."

Was he serious? Setha asked herself; her nerves were on edge whenever she was within twenty feet of the man. Khouri was walking sensuality. Either he had no idea of his effect on women or he had a fine idea and used it to his considerable advantage. The blare of a truck horn saved her from having to mull over the observation.

"The plumber," she said.

Khouri shortened the distance between them. "I'll see you in the morning." He propped her chin on his index and middle fingers, then trailed them along the curve of her jaw and felt the tension in her throat when she swallowed.

Setha turned to watch him leave the living room and make his way through the foyer where he let himself out.

Chapter 6

Clothes flew hither and yon across Setha's bedroom suite the next morning as she tried to decide on an appropriate outfit for her meeting at *Ross Review*. Actually, she wasn't as interested in selecting the *appropriate* one as she was in selecting just what would draw and hold Khouri Ross's beautiful eyes. The dress in hand would do that nicely, she thought, scrutinizing the chic creation. Though it was more suited for business attire, she also contemplated choosing the black pantsuit that flattered her butt.

The idea made her smile and she took note of herself. Losing interest in wardrobe selection, she cast aside the outfits and dropped to the bed holding her head in her hands. Flirting with a guy—even a guy as drop-to-the-knees gorgeous as Khouri Ross—was the last thing she needed on her mind.

How far could it go anyway once he realized her

newly acquired aversion to going out? Then there'd be questions—questions she had no answers for. She thought back to his concern over her home security system and it made her smile sadly. She couldn't add dogs or a guard at that point without raising her family's suspicions. That would seriously jeopardize her ability to get to the bottom of whatever the hell was going on.

She shook away the thought and conjured up a nicer one of Khouri Ross in her home. It was like he belonged there. She was so used to being at home alone, but his presence there yesterday…he didn't feel like a guest at all.

But business would be the last thing he'd want to discuss, remember? It didn't take much to decipher the meaning behind that. Was she ready to take it there if the opportunity presented itself?

That was a stupid question when only yesterday she was ready to beg him to do more than kiss her. And then what? Confess everything and have him put her under lock and key faster than her brothers ever would? She knew enough about Khouri Ross to know he'd certainly do exactly that.

"Dave, Noah, thanks for coming," Avra hurriedly greeted David Crus and Noah Eames when they arrived at her office for the meeting she'd requested.

"What's goin' on, Av?" Noah asked, pleasant as usual.

David was grinning. "Yeah, we don't usually get called over to this side of town," he teased, referring to the advertising department.

"Why haven't you released the news about the immigrant victims being Melendez employees?" she asked, in no mood for small talk.

"Well, it's..."

"We, um..." Noah exchanged a panicked look with David.

"Are you at least aware of it?" She snapped her fingers when there was more hesitation from the skilled reporters.

"We knew," David admitted.

Avra asked no further questions and simply spread her hands in a silent request for more information.

"Mr. B told us to hold it back," Noah confessed.

"Why...? Hey?" she blared when they hesitated again.

"We don't know, Avra."

"And we weren't about to question him on it."

Avra's coffee-brown stare shifted back and forth between the two men. "Anything else you're *holding back?*"

Yet again, Noah and David passed uneasy looks between one another.

"Dammit! *Now,* please!" Avra exploded, fists balled at her sides.

"We were tipped off—Wade Cornelius."

Her eyes narrowed. "Did my father know?" she asked when she was capable of speaking again.

"No," the men answered in unison.

Avra waved her hands to urge them out then she called out to them when they were halfway to the door, "What'd my dad mean when he told you to follow the money?"

"He wasn't clear on that," David said. "The killings

were definitely pro hits. Mr. B thinks maybe some-body's targeting MM."

Noah piped up next. "That's why we think he wanted us to hold off on revealing what we'd found."

"And what about you two? Do you think someone's targeting Melendez for whatever reason?"

"It's a path worth checking out."

Avra grimaced over Noah's response. "Anything to protect the good name of Melendez," she muttered. "Thanks, guys. You can go."

Walking circles around her office, Avra processed her suspicions. "John Holloway." She spoke the name as if it held some special power.

The topic of Wade Cornelius's last story with the *Review;* John Holloway was a former Machine Melendez employee who'd committed suicide—or at least that was the *story* everyone believed. Avra tapped her fingers to her chin and remembered. Wade and her father had a huge fight following the story's publication. Then Wade quit. After decades of friendship and partnership with Basil, he just quit.

As far as Avra knew, the two of them hadn't spoken since.

"What the hell is going on?" she whispered.

"Good morning, Ms. Melendez," Marta greeted Setha when she arrived for her meeting with Khouri.

"You probably won't be in the office long today anyway," Marta explained once they'd exchanged pleasantries.

"Oh?" Setha finished pulling the teal scarf from her neck. "Why's that?"

"He likes to work elsewhere when he's got things on his mind."

"Like what?"

Marta opened the office door. Her bracelets jingled when she waved Setha inside. "I probably shouldn't say."

Setha looked disappointed but didn't press the issue. Instead, she sighed and fixed Marta with a steadier expression. "I was sorry to hear about Wade Cornelius. I know he'll be missed around here."

"He was such a great man, even greater reporter," Marta drawled while reminiscing over her former colleague. "He will be missed but I doubt there'll be much outward lamenting after the way he left."

Setha followed Marta through the office as the woman rushed around tidying things. "Not such a good time, huh?"

"Hmph, *that's* understating it, hon. Him and Basil had an awful fight over his last story."

"Got it. Differences of opinion can start some knockdown, drag-outs."

"It was a lot more than that," Marta rambled absently while going through a stack of mail left forgotten along the windowsill behind the desk. "I think Wade was just tired of making a sow's ear look like a silk purse and I—" She blinked, glancing up and around the room as though she realized she was saying far too much.

"You just make yourself comfortable, Ms. Melendez." Marta returned the mail to the sill and headed for the door. "Khouri'll be out shortly."

Setha didn't try persuading more from the woman. Once Marta had made her hasty exit, Setha cursed acknowledging the fact that any attempts to find out more would likely end up the same way. Clearly Marta realized who she was talking to and clammed up. Chances were, any other employees would follow her example. Mulling over an answer to her dilemma was stifled when the office door opened again.

"Good morning," Khouri greeted with a wave and a teasing wink. "How's your toilet?" He savored the sound of her responding laughter.

She nodded. "Everything's fine, thanks for asking."

The mood grew heavier as silence made its presence known. Khouri's bright eyes took their time charting a leisurely trail along her body in the curve-clinging black suit and the matching short-waist jacket. Teal piping trimmed the jacket and flirty uneven hem of the skirt. Khouri made no effort to mask the intensity or the interest lurking in his gaze.

Setha, holding her portfolio now, gave it a quick shake near her legs where his eyes were focused then. "Maybe we should get started?" she asked.

Khouri merely waved, leaving it up to Setha to choose a place to get settled. She debated but a moment, before deciding that one of the chairs right near the desk would be better—safer.

Khouri stroked the light beard shading his jaw, in order to hide his smile at her avoidance of the living area. He took his place in the chair next to her instead of sitting behind his desk.

Setha cleared her throat, making a stab at finding her notes. She was, of course, far more preoccupied with observing him. Her dark, luminous gaze harbored a helpless quality while she watched him roll his sleeves over muscle-corded forearms. His eyes shifted her way as he did so.

Setha shook her head and opened the portfolio. "Sam's takes on the campaign are obviously pretty, uh, raw and basic but I think we may be able to use 'em. They could stand a bit of *softening,* though."

Khouri caught the edge of one of the racy pictures and tugged it from the portfolio sleeve. "Yeah." He brought his elbows to his knees while studying the glossy. "A 'softer' reaction might be the way to go."

Eager to share her ideas, Setha got comfortable in the chair. Kicking off her pumps, she curled her feet beneath her and reached over to hold a corner of the photo Khouri had taken. The shot captured a bikini-clad woman, bent over a convertible above the slogan: *Count on Machine Melendez parts for a good ride.*

"I think we could keep the woman, but have her seated on the hood of the car while she's looking out at a view of the ocean. Probably a sunset view—and she could maybe have a light blanket wrapped around her body—we could show a hint of shoulder." She brushed her fingers across the teal trim near her shoulder. "Maybe a little thigh, show her hair lifting against the breeze…"

Setha continued the idea, but Khouri had lost interest in the photo. Instead, he indulged in the beauty of her neckline and collarbone. A hint of her thigh was visible by the cut of the business suit she'd worn for the meeting. He was tuning back into her words just as she voiced her thoughts on the slogan.

"…and we could just tweak that—give it a less suggestive meaning. Let the customer know that MM parts will take them wherever they want to go and back. What do you think?" She waited a few beats and then let go of the photo and eased up a little. "Khouri?"

"Come with me," he said next, leaving his chair before she could reply.

Setha stepped into her shoes and quickly followed him to a far corner of the office. When an elevator arrived, she blinked and her lips parted. Uncertainty was on the heels of her surprise, but she felt silly hesitating and followed him into the car.

The ride was quietly…tense. Setha kept her eyes on the floor the whole time. His stare on her skin felt as potent as a physical touch. When she thought her anticipation would send her heart pounding right out of her chest, the elevator bumped to a stop.

The oak-paneled doors eased open and Setha forgot her agitation and almost everything else. They stood on the rooftop where a devastating Houston view awaited them. The day was set to be a sunny one and beams of the orange-golden light winked at them between the clouds and the scrapers outlined against the sky.

Setha walked across the brick-laid top as though she were in a daze. Mouth opened in amazement, she could scarcely form words. "This is…"

Khouri chuckled and pressed a thumb to his cleft chin as he savored her reaction. "Surely you've seen views like this at Melendez?"

Setha shook her head, wide coal-colored eyes still focused beyond. "Never like this…" she admitted.

Easing both hands into the pockets of his walnut-brown trousers, Khouri looked toward his shoes. "Happy I could please you," he said without looking her way.

Slowly, Setha looked away from the view and turned. "Why'd you bring me here?"

Looking up at her finally, Khouri kept his hands hidden while strolling toward her. "What you said gave me an idea—" he shrugged "—hope you don't mind me adding my two cents?"

"No." She shook her head in an eager manner.

Khouri's gaze narrowed against the sun when he took in the view. "There're all these great scenes in and around Houston. It'd be great to use them as the background or foundation of these ads—emphasize that a person can go anywhere content that MM parts will get 'em there and back."

"Khouri…" Setha brought a hand to her forehead and turned back to the scene at hand. "I love it and it's the perfect tie-in to what I've been saying." She smirked and fixed him with a saucy look. "You're pretty good at listening to women, Mr. Ross."

"Hmph." Khouri glanced toward his shoes again. "You can thank my sisters for that."

"So, um, what's next?" she asked before the captivating quality of his eyes caused her to swoon.

"Well, since we've got our model, all we need now is to pin down the locales."

Setha's expression grew wary when he reached out to rub a lock of her hair between his fingers. "You mean the model in Sam's photos, right?"

"No."

"Khouri? No," she answered his unasked question. "You're crazy," she said when he continued to leer at her.

At last, he nodded. "That may be true, but I think it's my best idea yet."

"Forget it."

"Don't tell me it doesn't excite you?"

How did he do that? Use this voice to instill such

lurid throbs inside her. She stepped back and gave one firm wave of her hand. "No way."

Khouri watched her coolly and then raised his hands in defeat. "Guess I'll have to settle for you helping me scout locales. You understand that means we've got lots of traveling ahead of us over the next few weeks?"

Setha blinked. "But we don't—"

"I expect you to come with me, Setha."

"I can't."

He leaned against the reinforced steel beams lining the rooftop. "Ms. Melendez, I can't accept a 'no' on this one."

"Why not?" She could barely hear her own voice.

Khouri focused on brushing his thumb across the silver links of his watchband. "I only allow one 'no.' You've used yours."

She would've laughed had her heart not been flipping from her throat to her stomach.

"Think how disappointed our dads will be to know *we* can't work together, either. Damn." He began to massage his jaw then. "I'd sure hate to break that to 'em."

"You wouldn't." She eyed his smug look warily. "You wouldn't let all this hinge on whether or not I'll come with you? You would," she answered when his expression remained unchanged.

"Fine," she obliged with a none-too-gentle slap to her thighs.

"Good." Khouri pushed off the railing and moved close to her. "Now are you sure I can't change your mind about being my model?"

Her head tilted just a fraction out of confusion. Just

then, she wasn't sure if he meant modeling for *Ross Review* or for him personally.

"Um—yes. Yes, I'm sure." She swallowed.

Khouri trailed his index finger around the piping at her jacket sleeve. "And there's nothing I can do to change your mind?"

The sun was starting to feel unbearably hot. Or perhaps it was just her. She wanted to melt. "You're welcome to try." Was that *her* voice?

"Thanks," he whispered seconds before his mouth slanted across hers and applied the sweetest pressure.

Setha, unfortunately, had no patience for sweetness then. She'd thought of kissing him for days and met the pressure of his lips with her own. Eagerly, she worked to entice his tongue into playing with hers. Unfortunately, he didn't appear to be interested. She was so hungry for him, that it took some moments for her to grasp that he wasn't responding. Once realization hit, her cheeks burned from embarrassment and she jerked out of the embrace.

"Sorry," she gasped, viciously smoothing back wavy locks from her dark face. "I'm sorry, Khouri," she murmured, practically tripping over herself to get back to the elevators.

Chapter 7

Setha made a mad dash from the elevator and returned to Khouri's office. She went back to the desk and began shoving items into the portfolio she'd brought to the meeting. She stopped, pressing the back of her hand to her mouth.

Stupid! Khouri Ross was the last man she should be inviting into her bed.

A throat cleared, grabbing hold of her attention then. Setha saw a slender dark young woman across the room.

"I take it my brother's on the roof?" she said, curiosity sparkling in her eyes as she smiled knowingly.

"Yes." The confirmation came slowly as Setha frowned a bit and headed toward the woman.

She nodded. "Figures."

"Marta says he only goes up there when he's got something on his mind," Setha probed.

"Mmm…that's true and he's definitely got something on his mind."

"Setha Melendez." She extended her hand.

"Avra Ross. Thank you for taking over the account meeting."

Setha smiled and nodded slowly. "Not a problem."

"So everything's moving along all right?"

Setha placed her free hand over the one she shook with Avra. "Everything's fine. I promise you it's all gonna work out."

"You'll have to forgive me." Avra rolled her eyes. "I didn't mean to pry." The hint of a grimace curved her mouth then. "I'm sure your brother already told you what an ogre I am."

Setha couldn't help but laugh. "I can honestly say that I've never heard him call you an ogre."

"Ah, well then." Avra smoothed her hands across the seat of her tailored black linen capris. "Guess that's one of the many words he's yet to learn." She gave a look of phony regret then. "I shouldn't have said that."

Setha's laughter bubbled up again. "No, trust me, it's fine." It was refreshing to meet a woman who didn't think Samson Melendez was some kind of god. "I'm sorry," she said, blinking tears from her eyes as she struggled to put on a straight face.

"Forget it." Avra waved off the apology. "We need more laughter around here."

Setha reached out to squeeze Avra's elbow then. "I was sorry to hear about Wade Cornelius."

Avra covered Setha's hand where it rested on the sleeve of her tanned blouse. "Thanks."

"Guess it's hit everybody around here pretty hard."

Avra nodded. "No surprise. He was important to a lot of folks 'round here."

Setha bit her upper lip and debated only a second. "Marta said he didn't leave under the best circumstances—something about an argument with your dad."

"Ah, yeah." Avra closed her eyes. "It was a doozy."

"What happened? Marta made it sound like a difference of opinion?" Setha was past caring about decorum, the possibility of getting answers had her almost giddy with excitement.

Thankfully, Avra wasn't one to beat around the bush. "Wade was tired of making Machine Melendez look like a company for the people. My dad disagreed with his opinion."

Setha blinked and took a step back. A sense of dread merged in with her excitement. Sound coming from the elevator shaft told her Khouri was probably on his way down.

"Avra, I'd like to know more about this. Would you be willing to talk to me?" Setha's voice was rushed but soft.

Intrigued, Avra responded with a slow nod at first. "Call me here. They'll connect you to my office."

"Thank you." Setha squeezed Avra's arm again and then grabbed her scarf and rushed from the office just as the elevator dinged its arrival.

Avra spread her arms when the doors opened. "Not the woman you were expecting, I guess."

Khouri rolled his eyes. "Not in the mood, Av."

She laughed. "Oh, I'm willin' to bet you're definitely in 'the mood.'" She sobered when he slammed down a fist to his desk, causing everything there to jump.

"Khouri, I'm sorry. I am but—" she took a tentative step closer to the desk "—we really need to talk."

In spite of his mood, the tone of Avra's voice gave Khouri pause. "What's up?"

"The murdered workers are all Melendez employees."

"What?" His rich brogue carried a softer quality. "How do you know this?"

"One of Gwen's colleagues at the *Journal* has a contact at the police department." Avra planted herself on her preferred spot on Khouri's desk. "David and Noah know about it, thanks to Wade."

Khouri sat on the opposite edge of the desk then. "Wade?"

"And that's where the info well goes dry," Avra interjected before he could ask how the man found out.

"Does Dad know?" Khouri asked instead.

"David and Noah told him and he essentially told them to bury it and pursue a different lead. Hence his 'follow the money' suggestion."

"But why?"

"Oh, Khouri, please." Avra scooted off the desk and began to stalk around the office. "You know about Dad's soft spot for Melendez. The stories we run on that company are proof of that."

"So you think he knows more than he's saying?"

"God, I hope not." Avra curled her fingers into either side of her head. "No way he's gonna tell *us* 'yea' or 'nay.'"

"Right." Khouri stroked his whiskered jaw while moving behind his desk. "Melendez must know."

"Which begs the question of why someone would

target Melendez employees? Ones on the bottom rung of the totem pole at that?"

Khouri had no reply which was just as well. Avra's phone chimed; she was being summoned back to her end of the building.

"Thanks for letting me ramble, Khouri." She sprinted for the door. "We'll talk later."

"Yeah." His reply was barely there. When the door slammed, he turned his desk chair. His gaze settled to the portfolio Setha had left behind.

Machine Melendez occupied an impressive spread on the outskirts of Houston. An elaborately designed silver-toned mini-scraper housed administrative personnel and executives; the rest of the vast acreage was covered by an abundance of buildings of varying shapes and sizes. Each held specific departments of the conglomerate. Danilo Melendez didn't work from one of the lavish top-floor office suites but rather a spacious yet understated ranch house at the farthest corner of the compound.

Setha didn't see the cars belonging to any of her father's staff and guessed they were all out for lunch. She knew her dad kept a car at the main parking deck and that he often traveled across the spread by horseback.

"Daddy?" She saw no signs of a horse, but hoped she'd catch him anyway.

Inside the ranch house, she tossed her things to a credenza in the foyer and decided to wait around for a while. In the living room, she settled on a sofa and wiggled off the teal pumps that were starting to pinch her feet. A smile curved her mouth at the sight of the pictures cluttering the long sofa table.

Most were pictures of her and her brothers as kids, but it was the ones of her parents that captured and held her interest. She ran her fingers across their smiling images and felt a rush of emotions at the happiness radiating from their faces. She thought of their happy marriage that ended with Adele Melendez's death.

Pulling her fingers from the photo, Setha rested back on the sofa. She wondered if she'd ever have anything close to what her parents had shared and grimaced while answering her own question.

Not if her stalker had his way.

Danilo Melendez was a boisterous man in his late sixties, but he didn't look a day beyond his early fifties. When his children had lost their mother, they were all certain that their father was sure to follow her into the afterlife. It had been a persistent battle, getting him to live following the death of the woman he had adored. He'd managed somehow and never failed to praise his kids for making him want to live.

"Mi hermosa chica!" Danilo called out to his "beautiful girl" when he spied her on the sofa.

"Daddy." Setha ran into her father's ready embrace, laughing when he squeezed her tight. She pressed a kiss into his neck and took comfort in the fresh scent of outdoors that always clung to his skin.

"Mi belleza." *My beauty.* Danilo sighed, pulling back to scan his daughter's face. A tad of scrutiny filled his vivid onyx-colored orbs the longer he regarded her. "Had I known that putting you on the Ross business would prevent you from joining me for dinner, I'd have thought twice."

"Just a lot of things on my plate, Daddy." She

squeezed Danilo's hand where it cupped her cheek. "The *Review* business is really a very small part of it."

"Is that right?" Danilo's scrutiny deepened. "I asked you to handle this because you *weren't* busy." He grimaced. "Sam won't settle for anyone else being involved except you… Perhaps Pow or Lou—I could always have one of them—"

"Daddy, no." Setha squeezed her father's hands and gave them a little shake. "I'm not overworked, I promise. Just…a little more protective of my 'downtime' is all."

Nodding, Dan kissed the back of her hand. "That I can definitely appreciate. I thank you for taking time to see me then."

"Oh…" Setha pulled the man into another hug.

"So how's it going over there at Ross?" Dan asked, escorting Setha back to the sofa and then heading for the bar.

"Fine." She curled her feet beneath her and watched her dad at the bar. "I *am* a little curious about something, though."

"Tell me."

"It's about Wade Cornelius's death." She blinked when a heavy clatter of glasses rose from the vicinity of the bar. "Can I get that, Dad?"

Danilo was waving his hand to urge her to keep her seat. "Go on, *belleza*. What about Cornelius?" Absently, he brushed shards of broken glass into a wastebasket.

"Well, he wrote a lot of stories—stories about Melendez." Setha snuggled deeper into the overstuffed plaid sofa. "There's been some question about whether the *Review* reported on certain…goings-on at the company from a slanted perspective."

Dan laughed and quickly finished preparing the drinks. "And what would make you ask such things, *belleza?*"

"But it's true, isn't it?" She reached out to take the glass of ginger ale he passed her. "I mean, *Ross* never has a bad word to print about us." She studied the bubbles fizzing up in the drink. "Same can't really be said for other papers in the country, can it?"

Dan chuckled, leaning back and propping his boots onto the unfinished wood table before the sofa. "I can recall several favorable stories about Melendez—just in the past few months if you must know."

Setha shook her head, knowing where her father was headed. "Folks aren't always quick to run down charities 'specially when they're doing good work."

"Then here's to good work." Dan raised his glass in a toast and then sipped the scotch reverently. "What is it you want to know, sweetness?"

Studying the ginger ale, Setha considered her words. "Are there things *Ross* covered at a slant and could those things ever come back to haunt us?"

"Haunt?" Dan bellowed around a roar of laughter. "Now you've got me thinking that you have too much of this 'downtime.'"

She didn't share her father's amusement. "I've never been happier."

"But I'm concerned. So are *los hijos*." He reached over to smother her free hand beneath his. "We can all tell that something's…off with you."

Setha drank down over half the ginger ale. "Now *I* can tell that you've been spending too much time around Sam. You're starting to sound just like him."

Dan took her glass and set it on the coffee table along

with his own. He next reached for her arm and made her face him. "We miss our bubbly girl. A family of gruff men needs that sweet element to remind us of the important things."

Setha's expression reflected cool understanding. "I know for a fact that your *hijos* have lots of sweet elements to keep them occupied."

Dan's somber expression lasted only a second longer and then he was laughing. "All right then, *chica.* I'll back down." He gave her a slight tug. "I want you to come to me or your brothers if there's anything I need to know, understood?"

"Understood." She hesitated to make eye contact for a second or two. "Will you do the same?" She looked up in time to catch the flicker of something in Dan's eyes.

He smiled brightly and pulled Setha into a hug. "I will," he said.

A few acres down from where Danilo kept his ranch house/office, stood a range of barns and fields where a select group of Melendez racehorses grazed. Inside one of those barns, the Melendez brothers had drinks with Bradley Crest, Chief of Detectives for City of Houston.

"Is this one of the perks of bein' Chief of Ds, B? Or will you get any work done at all today?" Lugo Melendez inquired, a ready smile sparking his double dimples.

Brad tossed back his second bourbon and water. "This is like a late lunch, Lou. After this, I'll be headin' home for a shower and an early dinner."

Male laughter filtered up through the high rafters of the multilevel barn.

"There's your answer, little brother. It's definitely

one of the perks of the job," Paolo Melendez said when
the laughter showed signs of quieting.

The men enjoyed their drinks in silence for a while.
Samson broke into the mood once he'd finished his
second mug of Dos Equis.

"Anything new, B?" he asked.

The loaded question removed all traces of easiness
from Brad's face. The immigrant murders had cast a
definite shadow over the top levels of Machine Melendez. Sam, his father and brothers had forbidden their
department heads to reveal anything about the victims
being Melendez employees. It had worked for a while,
but not for long.

"I've got no idea where the leak came from." Brad
tipped his beige Stetson back on his head a few inches.
"Truth be told, it's probably better the employees know.
Make 'em a lil more cautious."

"Or a little more frantic." Paolo poured his second
bourbon and shrugged. "It'd help if the victims had
more in common besides bein' Melendez employees."
His gruff voice sounded rougher in the wake of agitation.

"Well, if there's anything more, we ain't sniffed it out
yet." Brad finished his drink. "Not to mention they're
all newly immigrated to the country. That don't help,
either—not much history to go on."

"What about before they left Melendez?" Sam asked.
"They at least have *that* in common."

"Right." Brad's response carried a hint of sarcasm.
"Aside from two girls waitressing, a guy who worked
as a mechanic, one as a bellboy and another as a cook,
nothing extreme stands out." He kicked at the barn's

dusty floor. "I'm afraid their most intriguing common-ality is working for MM."

"What about socially?" Lou asked, scratching at the line where his straight hair tapered. "Maybe they've gone out together."

"Good, but no. We've looked down that road," Brad told them. "We're confident that they never had social connections. Machine Melendez is so vast, those people could've worked there for years and never met once."

"There's something." Samson held the empty beer bottle by the neck and tapped it to his knee. "We're just not seein' it. For those kids to be targeted... It means something."

"We ain't givin' up on this, guys," Brad promised, understanding how heavily this weighed on one of the most powerful families in Texas.

Paolo approached Brad with his hand outstretched. "Thanks for comin' out, man."

Brad's grin triggered the laugh lines around his sky-blue gaze. "Never pass on a chance to take a swig from your daddy's prized bourbon."

"B." Sam remained seated, but reached out to clasp Brad's hand when he passed.

"So? What now?" Paolo asked once Lou left to walk Brad to his car.

"We need to find out who those kids were." Sam pitched the empty bottle into a tall rusted can that served as a wastebasket.

Paolo's gray-black stare narrowed toward the barn's entrance. "Brad talks like they were nobodies."

"They were somethin' to somebody. So we find out who," Sam said.

Chapter 8

Setha turned down her father's request to join him for a horse ride across the grounds. She spent the next half hour on the living room sofa, before strolling through the house. Her walk took her into Dan's office where she studied the endless fields beyond the window behind the maple claw-footed desk at the rear of the spacious room.

Gradually, her interest turned toward her immediate surroundings and she observed the room—the awards and accolades. So many honors…

She took a seat behind the desk and began a web search. Topic: Wade Cornelius's stories for the *Ross Review*. Setha spent another half hour or so pulling Cornelius's pieces on Machine Melendez. She took time to read the last story written by Wade just before he left the publication he had helped Basil Ross to create.

Printing out the story copy, Setha frowned over it in

a thoughtful manner before slipping it into her purse. She browsed other hits, only because Melendez was mentioned somewhere within the text. There was an obituary for a John Holloway—a former employee for Machine Melendez.

Retrieving the printed story from her purse, Setha studied it another few minutes. "John Holloway," she whispered. There was something, but she hadn't the patience to muddle through it at this point. Checking her watch, she printed the obit for later perusal, shoved everything into her purse and left the house.

"Hey, cowboy? Unless you need anything, I'm signin' out for the day."

"Nah, I'm good." Khouri kept the back of his chair turned toward his assistant.

"I know what's got you so prickly." Marta strolled into the office, leaning against the row of low oak file cabinets lining a portion of the back wall. "She certainly is a beauty and brains to go with it. No wonder you can't keep your mind on anything else."

"Marta—"

"It's about time, if you ask me. *Which,* I know you didn't," she said when he turned in his chair to face her. "I still say it's about time *you* were the one not knowin' which way is up. Lord knows you put enough poor girls in that frame of mind."

Khouri let his head rest on the high back of the chair.

"Nighty, night," Marta sang and sauntered from the office.

Khouri shook his head, thinking how much Marta's arrivals and departures reminded him of a tornado touching down and taking flight. Sighing low, he traded the desk chair for the sofa and resumed his thoughts of the meeting with Setha Melendez.

More accurately, he resumed his thoughts of the kiss with Setha. Even *more* specifically her kissing him. He knew he'd confused her with his reaction. He'd intended—hoped—she'd take the lead. Her actions told him she was as attracted to him as he was to her. That she wasn't keeping herself under lock and key for another man. The smirk coming to the seductive curve of his mouth then was arrogance personified. Aside from being a mild inconvenience, another man wouldn't have stopped him from going after her.

Going after and getting. He sat up then, thumbing through the portfolio she'd left behind. He was gone from the office moments later.

Setha Melendez had always been a nervous cook. This was not to imply that her cooking skills were poor. On the contrary, they were remarkable considering she was mostly self-taught. She'd learned by trial and error, using her father and brothers as guinea pigs for her various recipes.

Her efforts paid off in the best way. Unfortunately, being a great cook didn't come without a price. Setha cooked when she was nervous and she cooked a considerable lot. She'd been at home three hours already following the visit to her dad at Machine Melendez. The long breakfast nook counter was filled with an array of pies and cookies. *That* was only the first batch.

There was something missing—something about the unfolding mystery, her stalker and the deceased Wade Cornelius. Every instinct told her there was a

connection between Cornelius's last story and whatever it was that she'd stumbled into. She only needed
to find the link.

Khouri stopped his truck at a distance from Setha's
front door and observed the scene meeting his eyes.
She had told him that she lived alone, but the four…
five guys in her driveway looked very much at home.
They were all shirtless, simply attired in saggy denim
shorts while polishing two cars as music blared from
the speakers of each vehicle.

Resting an elbow to the open driver's-side window,
Khouri drew fingers through the glossy onyx-colored
curls cropped close atop his head. He used his other
hand to tug his tie free of his shirt collar and tried to
make sense of the scene. He straightened behind the
wheel when Setha arrived outside.

She linked her arms about the waists of two of the
young men, while the others ambled about. Then the
merry sextet made their way around the back of the
house. With a curious, albeit dangerous, smirk sharp-
ening his caramel-doused features, Khouri grabbed the
portfolio and headed for the back of the house, as well.

Conversation and laughter became heightened the
farther he traveled along the stone lane leading to the
patio. Khouri muttered a curse at the unlocked double
doors and made his way inside. He followed the raised
voices and laughter all the way to the kitchen.

He refused to acknowledge the sense of relief that
all the liveliness came from that area of the house as
opposed to the bedroom. Smirking then for a purely
different reason, he leaned against the high curving en-

tryway and watched Setha issuing heating instructions as she presented each young man with a pie.

"And tell your moms to give me a call, all right? Now, on your way." She accepted hugs and kisses from each of the boys.

Khouri watched the kids retrieve bikes parked on the deck outside the kitchen. He returned to observing Setha as she moved around the kitchen—wiping down counters, adjusting oven temperatures. Every so often, she stopped to mull over a folder on the kitchen table.

He knocked once on the doorway and waved when she whirled around.

"Khouri?" she breathed, eyes wide. "What—"

"Better question might be 'how did I get in?'" He braced off the doorway. "Don't folks in River Oaks lock their doors?"

"With a houseful of teenagers, such things are often overlooked. When they're here, I tend to lose track of time."

"Rowdy bunch." He smiled. "Yours?" he teased.

Amused, Setha rolled her eyes. "Kids of neighbors. I've known those guys since they were infants."

"It's no excuse not to lock your door, Setha." He tapped the portfolio to his pant leg. "It's exactly that type of forgetfulness an intruder would count on."

"Do you know you have a knack for instilling calm?" She rolled her eyes not so much out of amusement then.

"I can't help it." He easily blocked her path when she would have headed for the refrigerator. "Lock your doors."

The closeness and the softness of his voice only re- minded Setha of earlier that day on the rooftop of his office. She remembered the humiliation, the sting of it heating her cheeks.

"Why are you here, Khouri?"

He presented the portfolio she'd left behind.

She blinked. "Thanks. You didn't have to come all this way to return it. I could've gotten it at our next meeting."

Khouri put distance between them and went to lean against a counter. "I wasn't so sure about that after the way you ran out on me today."

"Hmph," she mumbled with a smile before she went to check the cookies baking in the top oven.

"What's funny?" he asked.

"Nothing. Trust me."

"Did I do something?" He faked confusion, knowing full well what the issue was.

Setha's laughter was a little more pronounced then. Her high ponytail slapped her cheeks when she shook her head. "You didn't do anything, Khouri. You didn't do anything at all, remember?" She let the oven door close with more force than was needed.

Khouri folded his arms over his chest. "Have you eaten?" He kept his eyes on his shoes—one crossed over the other. Another laugh was the response.

"I never eat when I get on a cooking kick."

"Well, hell, that's no fun. Come out with me."

"No, I, um…no." She couldn't decide whether she wanted her hands in or out of the denim capris she sported.

"Is that because there's someone you're trying not to upset?"

She opened the refrigerator door and then closed it. "There's no one."

"Does *he* know that?"

Setha blinked and turned from the refrigerator to study him curiously. "What are you talking about?"

Khouri maintained his spot along the counter. "You're starting to offend me. Turning down all my invitations."

She resumed wiping down the countertops, starting with the one nearest him. "You'll get over it," she grumbled.

"Don't be so sure," he said, moving from the counter and turning her against it.

He'd moved so quickly, she barely had time to register the change in her position. The only thing registering then was his mouth on hers. He delivered the kiss thoroughly, enticing her tongue into the sultriest of duels. Infrequently, he curved his tongue over and around hers and then traced the even ridge of her teeth which coaxed her to do the same to him.

"What are you doing?" She barely formed the words when he finally let her up for air.

"Giving you what you wanted earlier." He trailed his nose along the soft curve of her jaw and was kissing her again soon after.

It wasn't in Setha's nature to hold back, especially when she wanted something as much as she'd wanted to be kissed by Khouri Ross. Boldly, she tucked herself into his lithe, lean frame, participating in the kiss with an eagerness that made him rest against the counter while keeping her close.

His hands were everywhere since he'd wanted to touch her, unrestrained, from the moment he'd found her in his office. He cupped her bottom neatly encased in the denims and squeezed, drawing her into his firming erection. The fact that she didn't resist added hunger to his kiss. For some reason, it also warned him not to rush it.

Why he should care about that was unknown to him. It was all too clear that they both wanted what was happening. But she was a mystery to him—one he wasn't sure he'd ever fully solve.

He began to apply quick, supple pecks to her well-kissed mouth. "Sure you won't have dinner with me?"

"Mmm…" She ran her tongue across his perfect teeth. "Dinner's not what I want." The words spilled from her tongue and she instantly regretted them. Bristling, she muttered a criticism believing she'd done another fine job of humiliating herself.

Cupping her lovely molasses-dark face, he kissed her again. He let her hear the moans her sweet mouth drew from him. Setha treated herself to the feel of his body smoothing her hands across his wide back and shoulders and the chiseled expanse of his torso.

"Promise to lock up as soon as I leave?" he said when the kiss broke that time.

She snuggled closer to suckle his earlobe. "I promise to lock up…good and tight."

He couldn't resist another kiss then. His fingers skirted the button fly of her capris. When the exploring hand insinuated itself between her thighs, she squeezed them close and absorbed the sensation he provided.

Khouri used his free hand to weigh her breast. Her gasping moans were a pleasurable massage to his ego and he practically fondled her right out of the pink, capped-sleeved blouse she wore.

"Stop me, Setha."

"Why?" She was virtually straddling him on the

counter then. Her fingers were curled into his shirt and she resumed her hungry suckling of his tongue.

"Setha? Honey, I should go," he groaned when the words finally left his mouth.

She didn't try to entice him into changing his mind. Slowly, she unwrapped herself from him. "Night," she bid, moving back and keeping her eyes on his.

Khouri commanded his legs to carry him to the door. He was almost home free when she called out to him.

"It's apple," she said upon presenting him with one of the pies from the hutch.

He grinned. "This is a first."

She raised one shoulder. "Hopefully a good first?"

Provocatively long lashes fluttered down over his hazel stare. "You have no idea." He studied every inch of her face and then leaned close to kiss the corner of her mouth. He left her with the order, "Lock up."

Setha took care of every lock. Then she returned to the kitchen and indulged in a few deep, refreshing breaths.

"Yeah?"

"Where are you?"

"Pretty sure you know."

Silence drifted across the phone lines for a time.

"You've gone too far."

"You knew this would be our endgame."

"But not like this."

"*Hermano*…is this *you* talkin' or the money?"

"It's both and since the money *is* the money, it'd be in your best interest to take heed, as well."

"Bullshit. You think I care about money? I haven't

cared about money since we were cheated out of what's ours."

"At any rate, you're drawing too much attention too fast. Cornelius wasn't to be touched."

"It all started with him."

"He wasn't to be touched!"

Silence.

"Now you back off Setha Melendez or I won't be able to help you."

"They have to pay."

"And they will, but in a way that can't possibly be traced back to us."

"This is bigger than us, *hermano*. You know that. This *money man* wouldn't be giving us a second thought if it wasn't."

"Even still, we have a chance to come out of this set for life if we play the game right. Now can I count on you?"

"You can always count on me, *hermano*."

"And you're backing off the Melendez?"

"Backin' off."

The phone connection ended.

The man on one end of the call held on to his receiver and frowned. "For now," he said.

Chapter 9

The attendees at Wade Cornelius's funeral read like a who's who of Houston society. Out of a genuine respect for the man they admired, many journalists on hand put away their notepads and recording devices to share space with the politicians, executives and celebrities whose stories they craved. Everyone came to pay tribute to a man who had touched their lives in one form or another.

Setha had arrived with her brother Paolo. She stood taking in the mass of bodies covering the cemetery where Cornelius's body was about to be interred. She wondered whether her *follower* was there. It'd make sense for him to attend since everything she was uncovering was telling her that he was the reason for this particular event. She managed to shake away the morose thought just as Paolo ended his conversation with the business associate who'd pulled him aside.

Paolo tugged his little sister close and tweaked her chin. "You all right, girl?"

She made a pretense at straightening his tie. "You know, if one more person asks me that, I believe I'll scream."

"Sorry, darlin'." He took her hand and gave it a squeeze. "You gotta know we're concerned, though?"

"I know—" she squeezed back "—I'm sorry for snapping but really, Pow, I'm just peachy. Despite the fact that I'm about to walk through a cemetery."

Paolo's robust laughter drew more than a few smiles in spite of the gloominess of the occasion. Arm in arm, the siblings headed forward. Setha's eyes widened and her fingers curved a smidge tighter into Paolo's arm when she spotted Khouri surrounded by three women who were almost as tall as he was.

Setha recognized one of the women as Avra Ross and wondered if the others were the sisters Raquel and Fiona. Her mouth curved into a rueful smile. She'd hoped to speak with Raquel that night when she had tried to visit her club.

If that son of a b hadn't been tracking me, I might've been able to talk to her, Setha thought. She may've found someone to finally bounce her outrageous theories off of. Instead, she'd been chased barefoot down a slimy alley and forced to hide out in some stranger's car.

She gasped then, her free hand immediately going to her mouth. Paolo didn't pay much attention to her reaction.

"You say somethin', hon?" he murmured.

"Seth, that's crazy…" she told herself. "I, um, I think I see Daddy and them." She pointed across the grounds.

Once hugs and handshakes were exchanged between

the Melendezes, talk stirred regarding the various attendees. The guys remarked on the information they'd gotten out of Brad Crest.

"He seemed certain no one out of his office let it spill about the vics being Melendez employees." Lugo tapped his fingers against his silver-and-black speckled tie. His deep-set browns roamed the cemetery grounds with blatant suspicion.

"We might come through this without the high-level execs spillin' the beans on that. That happens, chances are we could avoid a panic," Paolo added.

Sam tapped fingers to his dimpled chin and observed his brothers stoically. "You two are whistlin' in a shitty wind if you think that'll happen. Everybody, high-level to custodial, they've been whisperin' about this since day one."

"At least we've got that much to go on." Paolo's slanting dark stare remained downcast. "Maybe them being Melendez employees *is* why they were targeted."

"*Mis hijos,* I think we should let this rest." Danilo had been listening to his sons' theories. He clapped Paolo's shoulder and gave it a squeeze beneath the worsted fabric of his navy suit coat. "Let the police do their jobs, yes?"

Samson and Setha left off with the speculating, Paolo and Lugo didn't quite agree.

"The guy behind this is a complete nutcase," Lugo declared. "We're fools to believe he's done with this spree of his."

"You got that right," Paolo said.

"Do you even realize that you're upsetting your sister? *Basta.*" *Enough,* he urged, having noticed when Setha closed her eyes and swallowed.

"I'm fine, Daddy."

Dan shook his head. "I say we change the subject."

Setha eased both hands into the pockets of the black jacket which complemented the chic A-line dress she wore. "It seems that Basil Ross and the deceased parted ways with a disagreement between them."

Danilo's expression reflected surprise.

"They had a terrible argument." Setha's smile was barely there as she watched the breeze lift her father's thick black hair off his wide forehead. "Wade Cornelius resigned right after that." She pressed her lips together, feeling Dan's astute gaze boring into her. Undaunted, she still selected her next words carefully.

"It's *rumored* that the fight had something to do with his last story—the suicide of a man that worked for us."

Setha's revelation was accentuated by a faint chime that drew the crowd's attention to the grave site. Paolo and Lugo moved ahead while Setha and Dan strolled arm in arm. Samson lagged behind his family and watched his sister.

The cemetery began to clear following a dramatic rendering of "Amazing Grace" from the choir of the Cornelius family's church. Avra was conducting a search into the depths of her black tote while heading in the general vicinity of the parking area. Her slow trek was blocked when she bumped into the wall that was Samson Melendez. She took a step back and glowered.

"What rock did you crawl out from under?"

Sam's grin had the capacity to make him look at ease and dangerous at once. "I came to pay my respects."

"Understandable." Avra smirked, taking the sunglasses from their perch atop her head and exchanging it for one across her nose. "After all, Wade Cornelius almost single-handedly gave Melendez its sterling rep. Not an easy thing to get in this town."

"We're very proud of our sterling rep." Something had cooled in Sam's dark, riveting eyes.

"And are you referring to your *real* rep or the one Wade created for you?"

"Are you saying he reported inaccurately?"

"Lord, Sam." Avra eased the shades down a smidge on her nose. "Have you ever even read any of the man's stories on Melendez or...*had* them read to you?" She set the shades back in place and folded her arms over the chic scoop-neck dress she wore. "Anyone with a brain would know they were slanted to favor Melendez."

"You are includin' your daddy there, Av? Are you saying that Basil Ross would allow false stories to be printed in his paper?" He made a tsking sound. "Don't sound like the Basil Ross I know."

"'Scuse me," she said. She proceeded to step around him then.

Sam prevented it. "I heard they had a falling-out—your dad and the deceased. Maybe over one of his last stories on the Machine."

"Get out of my way, Sam."

Ignoring her thoroughly peeved request, Sam moved closer, easily crowding her. "Why so edgy, Av? That kind of tension's bad for one's health, you know? You should do somethin' about that."

Her smile bordered on a sneer. "And I'll bet you've got tons of ideas that could help me out, hmm?"

He moved in so close then that the brim of his black

Stetson provided her with ample shade from the sun. Avra prayed he couldn't see the unease—or anticipation—stirring behind her sunglasses.

His wide mouth, set appealingly beneath a neatly trimmed mustache, tilted upward into the most seductive of smiles. "I've got ideas that could keep you busy for weeks," he taunted.

Avra chose not to acknowledge the reaction his words roused.

"'Scuse me," she repeated, then darted past him and bolted.

Paolo had gotten caught up in another conversation once the funeral ended which gave Setha time to sign the attendance book while she waited. She'd signed her name but kept the pen poised, biting her lip as she debated. Then, following her instincts, she flipped back the pages in order to scan the names already entered. A few names stuck out to her, her pen hovering over them for a moment or so. The study of the names, and everything else for that matter, flew from her brain when she felt a faint tug at her dress sleeve. Khouri Ross stood behind her.

"Hey." She swallowed. Her greeting was breathless as she fought to make her mind work.

Khouri kept his hold on her short sleeve, rubbing the fabric between his fingers. "So you *do* come out in public and to funerals no less. Should I be concerned?"

Setha laughed and missed the way his eyes followed the toss of her hair.

"If what I've learned is true, my family owed a lot to Mr. Cornelius." When his sleek brows joined, she changed the subject. "I saw you with Avra. You guys were talkin' to two other women…"

"My sisters," he confirmed, tilting his head when she pressed her lips together and nodded. "Did you think otherwise?"

A little wave of humor funneled up inside her. "You'll never know," she sang.

"Right." He scanned the thinning crowd while jingling the keys in his pocket. "Walk you to your car?" he offered.

"Oh…Khouri, thanks, but I came with Paolo. We'll be leaving as soon as he's done talking."

"Mmm-hmm…" Khouri nodded while pulling a mobile phone from his back pocket.

Setha frowned a bit, watching him work with the phone as though she wasn't even there.

"Pow?" he said, staring at Setha. "Khouri Ross. What's goin' on?"

Setha's lips parted.

"Right, right…yeah, I'm here—actually standin' with your sister…right. Listen, we've got some business to discuss so I'll make sure she gets home and has dinner, all right? Mmm-hmm…yep…sounds good. See ya 'round."

"Khouri, I can't—"

"Don't bother." He slipped the phone back inside one pocket and withdrew keys from another. "It's fine with me if you prefer going home and cooking me dinner instead of going out."

The man's slow, easy confidence had her torn between wanting to laugh and wanting to swoon.

"If anybody ever told you that you were subtle, they lied."

"What?" He feigned confusion with raised brows. "We're just goin' to talk a little business. What's wrong with that?"

Laughing softly, Setha studied the strappy heels she wore. "Nothing's wrong with that, but I distinctly remember you telling me that you don't discuss business during dinner."

"Aah." Khouri took her upper arm and began leading her from the cemetery. Pulling her close, he brought his mouth a breath away from her ear. "Good of you to remind me of that."

Had she any idea of how long she'd linger in her foyer later that afternoon, she would have left pillows and blankets there.

Setha had scarcely set her lock when Khouri had her in his arms and was kissing her out of every scrap of clothing she wore. His method was as easy as his manner. He took so much time with her that she wanted to scream for him to give her what she craved the most.

Eventually, she settled for pounding her fists to his back and nudging her hips to his to relay her desires.

"Wait for it..." he coaxed, tonguing his way down, over and around her plump, lace-covered breasts.

He subjected her to double caresses of every sort—kissing her deep while massaging the hem of the dress up over her thighs—unhooking her bra while stroking her nipples through the fabric.

Setha couldn't recall when pleasure had last visited her so exquisitely. She realized that she couldn't recall because it had *never* visited her so exquisitely.

She pushed the jacket from his back and unbuttoned his shirt, but he captured her wrists and prevented her from doing more. Still, she strained against his hold and then submitted and watched her nails graze the unyielding breadth of his caramel-toned chest. She waited, not against letting him have his way.

Khouri took great advantage of her decision. Suckling her earlobe, he brushed his fingers across the lavender bikini-cut panties she wore and grazed the hypersensitive nub of desire at the apex of her thighs.

The simple caress carried her toward the brink of an orgasm. Without shame, Setha cried out into his shoulder and squeezed her thighs tight about his fingers. Soon after, she felt the foyer's cool checkerboard flooring against her bare bottom. Her panties clung to one slender ankle along with one sheer stocking—the other had been tossed aside.

Without effort, Khouri lifted her and replaced her on his dark suit coat. He took her out of the dress and bra seconds later. Then, he stopped and took time to worship the texture and complexion of her skin—her body.

Setha bit down on her lip, lashes fluttering on the nervousness swirling within. The nervousness had nothing to do with fear but anticipation. The way he watched her, she wondered if he was trying to decide which part of her to feast on first.

He decided. His hands covered her breasts. Setha felt her entire body shiver in reaction. His thumbs rubbed across the firming nipples until they puckered up out of the dark mounds. He maintained the caress even as he lowered his head to her thighs and again manipulated the sensitized nub that sent pleasure lancing through her. The fact that his tongue stirred the throbbing desire had Setha arching instinctively into the oral treat that he delivered.

She couldn't make up her mind whether to rake her fingers through his hair or hers. She decided on threading her fingers through the cropped curls—the move allowed her to direct the tilt of his head as he took her to the threshold of climax for a second time.

"Khouri…" she sobbed when he pulled away that time. Blindly, she reached out for him only to feel his hand on hers before he pressed a kiss to her palm. "Jackass," she hissed.

He had the nerve to grin while watching her pout. Rising above her, he slowly unfastened the cuffs of the dark shirt and pulled it from his back.

Setha noticed the condom he took out of his pocket and she pulled him down into a throaty kiss that he was totally unprepared for. She kissed him hungrily, stroking his tongue and entwining it about hers. All the while, she worked at the fastening of his trousers.

Khouri was undone by the mastery of her kiss. It didn't register that she'd freed his erection and applied the condom, until he felt her nails raking his bare butt.

"Setha…hell." He wouldn't waste time removing his pants and took her in one long thrust.

She whimpered instantly—eagerly going to work winding herself along his enviable length. Her lips formed a small O as she took him. He felt like sheer heaven, filling her, hitting every intimate spot inside her core.

Khouri rested his head on her shoulder, relishing the tight, creamy heat that gloved him. He changed the direction of his thrusts and smiled weakly at the sound of her whimpers changing over to moans. Regaining control, he placed a hand over each thigh which opened her more fully to his drives. He claimed her at his leisure and didn't allow her much room to move when it was obvious that she wanted to lock her legs around his back.

Setha rested her arms above her head. Already pert, full breasts moved to a more prominent position. Khouri couldn't resist tugging one into his mouth, devouring the dark-chocolate-dipped nipple as he groaned.

Total bliss engulfing her, Setha shivered when he finally let her wrap her legs around his waist. She drew him deeper, clenching her walls around him, keeping him where she wanted him and sighing her approval.

In time, their movements became frenzied. The rapacious fire between them filled the foyer with sounds of release and satisfaction.

Chapter 10

Khouri's approving smile deepened when he snuggled into the bed coverings. He could hear the change in Setha's breathing and knew she was awake.

"Floor's nice—this is better," he groaned. When there was no comment, he opened an eye and looked her way. "What?"

Setha lazily trailed her fingers through his hair. "Your cologne…it's very nice."

His bright sleep-sexy gaze narrowed. "Thanks," he murmured.

"It's different. I can't quite place it."

"It's not easy to find." He snuggled back into the pillow and grazed his fingers down the bare arm closest to him on the pillow. "I get it from this specialty shop down in Kemah."

Setha nodded, studying her hands folded in the middle of a pillow. She'd been resting on her elbows and watching him as he slept.

"Well, it's really nice." She stroked the long silky hairs of his brows. "I think I've only smelled it on one other guy."

Eyes closed, he produced a lazy smile. "Oh, yeah?"

"Mmm-hmm." She laughed softly then. "I don't even know his name." She risked a look at Khouri whose eyes were still closed. "Guess you could say he came to my rescue...."

Khouri opened his eyes then, but watched her in silence over the span of several seconds. "When was this?"

"A few weeks ago."

"At a club?"

Her breath caught and she broke eye contact. "Yeah...your sister's club—behind it, actually."

"Who was he, Setha?"

She squeezed her eyes shut tight. "Why didn't you say anything?"

"At first, I thought I was crazy." He rubbed his eyes. "But there was no mistaking you—'specially after you came to my office." He looked up at her then. "When did you know it was me?"

"I forgot about the cologne. When I saw you at the funeral with your sisters..." She flexed her fingers against the pillow. "Raquel is the one who owns the club, right?" She took his smile for confirmation. "And then there's your car... Is that why you gave me a ride today?"

His smile turning wicked, Khouri looked under the sheet at her bare form beneath. "That is definitely *not* why I gave you a ride today. Who is he?"

He repeated the question before she could smile over his suggestive words. "It's complicated," she said.

A muscle flexed along Khouri's jaw when his stare faltered. "Did you— Do you love him?"

"What? No. No, it—it's not like that. Not that at all." She almost laughed at the absurdity of it.

"Then what is it?" His slow-to-rise temper was beginning to simmer.

"I—"

"Setha, believe me when I say that I plan on askin' 'til I get an answer. A good one."

She blinked, understanding that he meant what he said. "This is bigger than me, Khouri, and it's got nothing to do with a love affair gone bad."

He caught her wrist when she shifted between the covers. "Why won't you tell me? Don't you trust me? Because I damn well don't buy that you go to bed with guys you don't trust."

Setha stretched the hand above the wrist he held and smoothed it across his jaw. "You're so much like my brothers that it's scary."

"Jesus, Setha." He massaged the back of his free hand across the frown forming at his brow. "What the hell does that mean?"

"If they knew what I was doing, they'd bully, badger and crowd me 'til I backed off and let them handle it." Heavy tufts of wavy dark hair curtained her face when she bowed her head. "I have to see this through. I know too much not to see it through."

Khouri muttered another curse while pushing himself up against the headboard. "People say I'm the 'laid-back' one of my family. I guess they think I have to be to handle women like my sisters unless I want to get run over." His easy smile faded when he looked Setha's way. "But folks soon come to realize that it's not wise to make me angry. This is precisely what you're doing right now."

She shook her head resolvedly. "I can't…tell you." She scooted to her knees before he could explode and held his face in her hands. "I have to show you."

Danilo was just rounding the bar when his guest arrived. "Thanks for coming, Bas."

"You made it sound urgent," Basil Ross said once he exchanged a handshake with his old friend.

"Wouldn't you agree in light of everything going on lately?"

Basil pulled off his black suit jacket. "Are we talkin' Wade's death or—"

"We're talking Wade's death and the death of my employees."

Basil sipped the Courvoisier Dan handed him. "You think it's all connected?"

"Has to be."

Basil began to walk a path around the room with its early evening view of the Melendez prized horses. "The murders have been professionally handled—that's obvious."

Dan's hand paused over a bottle of Hennessey. "How do you know that?"

"They're too clean." He tasted more of the drink. "Won't be long before the press decides to announce the connection between the victims and Machine Melendez."

"Why do you think they haven't done that yet?"

"Well, I know why *my* staff hasn't." Basil's piercing

hazel stare reflected confident authority that gradually merged into something a bit more suspect. "I can only think of one reason the others haven't. It doesn't take a genius to see *Ross Review* has a soft spot for Melendez. If these murders turn out to be a storm for the Machine, it could be said that *Ross* was covering for you." He scratched at the baby-fine hair along his temple. "I don't even want to think about the repercussions of that."

Cradling his glass in both hands, Dan sat on the corner of an armchair. "You think the murderer has ties to MM?" His handsome copper-toned face was a picture of disbelief.

"I pray that's not the case." Basil stared into the contents of his glass before tossing it all back. "But you know as well as I do that a lot of bad history has gone into the forming of both our companies. Whether or not the murders are a part of that doesn't dismiss the fact that there are horrors we can be tied to—even to this day."

"Basil." Dan left the arm of the chair. Awkwardly he tugged the black-and-gold suspenders from his broad shoulders while holding on to his glass of Hennessey. He settled down into a chair this time. "The kids can never find out about any of that."

"Naive to think none of it will ever come out." Basil set his empty glass on the oak bar top. "Maybe it's time for us to pay the piper."

"You think there could be blackmail?"

"It'd make sense." Basil stroked the flawless mocha-colored skin covering his jaw. "'Specially if this really does have to do with something ugly from our pasts.

There've been five murders already, Dan, and no one's come to us with any demands."

Somewhat pacified by that fact, Dan sipped his drink. "Why?"

"Because that would mean whoever's behind this isn't after money." Basil went to stand before the windows. "And *that* would mean that this is very personal."

Over coffee and a plate of cookies—from her baking spree earlier that week—Setha told Khouri how her present situation began.

"Carson Arroyo." Cradling a warm mug in her hands she sat cross-legged in the tangled bed and told him about the young man who had visited her office one day.

"I was out of town. My staff said he had insisted on speaking to me even though he was obviously troubled." For several seconds her nails tapping the ceramic mug were the only sounds in the room. "I got the message he left when I returned from my trip. Same day, I get a call from a man asking about this same guy. He was set on finding out what the guy said to me and sounded kind of put out when I had to tell him, more than once, that I wasn't even here when the guy came by."

"A hard-to-convince type," Khouri noted, muscle-corded arms folded over his broad chest while he leaned back against the pillows at the headboard.

"Hmph. And then some." She sipped at her coffee and then reached over for one of the large manila folders that were held together by a fat rubber band which she pulled off. Shuffling through the contents, she located a pink message slip which she handed to Khouri.

"No number?" He waved the ticket noting the mysterious visitor.

"He came to the office the same day I got back—like he knew I was there."

Khouri's eyes narrowed. "Has he been following you since then?"

Setha drew up her legs and set her chin to a knee. "It'd make sense but it was still a while before I put it all together. I couldn't see why someone who wanted me dead would introduce himself much less want me to know what he looks like."

"All kinds of fools in this world, darlin'," Khouri murmured, while studying the message slip. "Maybe he doesn't want you dead." His brilliant stare traveled with meaning across her face and body.

Setha shook her head and smiled self-consciously. "I'm pretty sure he's not in love with me."

Did the woman ever look into a mirror? Khouri asked himself, observing her bare, licorice-dark legs peeking out from beneath the hem of his shirt. "Why is that so hard to believe?" he asked.

"Because there's more."

"There'd have to be." He looked toward the second hefty folder on the bed.

Setha put her mug on the nightstand and then scooted toward the folder. "This is where it gets complicated."

"You're kidding?"

Grinning, she nudged her foot against his calf in payback for the sarcasm. "Did you know all the victims in those immigrant worker murders were Melendez employees?"

Khouri's jaw muscle flexed. "I heard that."

From the folder, Setha retrieved what looked like a news article. "Look at this."

"*Ross Review,* May 1986?" he noted.

"Check the byline."

"Wade Cornelius." He pushed up against the pillows lining the carved pine headboard and scanned the article with a keener eye.

"Apparently there was a suicide. A man named John Holloway—a former Melendez employee."

"Honey, what—"

"Just wait." Setha scooted to her knees and extended her hands. "Just bear with me a few more seconds, all right?

"I got that article from Carson Arroyo," she continued when the tension relaxed in Khouri's shoulders.

"What'd he tell you?"

"Marveled about the office—" her hands fell to her lap "—went on and on about the building—asked me what kind of charities we handled and whether MM offered protection to the families of fallen workers. Before I could explain what we did, he gave me the article along with a photo of a billboard ad." She returned to the folder and withdrew the shot.

PROTECTING WORKERS AND THEIR FAMILIES THE MACHINE MELENDEZ WAY!

"He asked me if we protected the families of workers believed to have committed suicide." She moved to the head of the bed and leaned against Khouri. "I finally got the sense that the guy was more than someone in need of a hot meal. One of my staff came into the office and he just left. Didn't take the article or the other papers in the folder he had brought. Since that day, I've been trying to find a connection between that ad, that story and Carson Arroyo."

"Have you told any of this to the cops?"

"Are you crazy? My brothers would find out then for sure."

"And this is a bad thing?"

"Khouri, I have to know what this is. Can't you understand that?"

"Not if it means your life." He caught her wrist when she moved. "Have you already forgotten the son of a b who chased you down an alley?"

She gave a noticeable shiver. "I could never forget that."

He relaxed his hold. "That night. Why were you there?"

She gave a sad smile. "I wanted to talk to somebody who knew Wade Cornelius. It was obvious that he was writing slanted stories in favor of my dad's business. I didn't know what kind of man that made him so I decided to start by speaking to the people who may've known him best." She tossed back hair from her forehead. "I couldn't risk going to the *Review* with Samson working there with Avra—thought I could make an *in* with Raquel and start some sort of dialogue but I ran into you instead."

She moved closer and pressed a fist into the center of his chest. "Please don't say anything."

"Hell, Setha." He rolled his eyes.

"I think I'm close, Khouri." She flattened one hand to his chest and the other to her own. "I'm closer than I've ever been before. I know it."

"Doesn't make me feel better knowin' that."

"Look, Khouri. Carson Arroyo's name was on that attendance list at the funeral today."

"Son of a b," Khouri hissed and left the bed. "Guy's not only psychotic, he's stupid, as well," he muttered.

Setha moved into the spot Khouri had vacated. "I think he knows exactly what he's doing."

Khouri stopped just short of the master bath. "Because he signed the attendance book?"

"I think he has a statement to make. He wants everyone to *know* he's doing this and the only way we have a chance in hell of stopping him is to find out *why* he's doing it."

Chapter 11

The next morning found Setha in the midst of another cooking spree. She wasn't suffering from a case of nerves, though, more like a case of happiness. She knew it was too soon to feel such bliss, but the feeling was there and there was no denying that. Would it go beyond that? she wondered. If her not-so-secret admirer kept turning up like a bad penny, she couldn't be sure.

Khouri was already out of bed, but didn't let his hostess know that. Instead, he took a remote spot at the rear of the kitchen and watched her move around the space as she cooked. Since the day they'd met— *officially* met—he'd been telling himself that he was only so infatuated because of the circumstances of their first meeting. Then, he was telling himself that it was because she was so damn good to look at. While those reasons definitely had their merit, he now knew that there were lots more.

He'd always told his sisters to let the guy get to know the person *inside* before rushing into the physical part. That was simply a ploy to protect their virtue. Personally, he'd never taken the time to get to know a woman on the inside—never really cared about it. The woman never seemed to care, either, so all was well.

Then, Setha Melendez literally barreled into his world and he found himself reevaluating all he thought was right. There was so much more he wanted to know about her. What he already knew had him craving her company to the point of obsession. Approaching her at the funeral had nothing to do with coaxing information about her pursuer and everything with wanting to simply be with her.

Bowing his head, Khouri brought his hands to his face and sighed. He had to at least try at snapping out of whatever spell she had cast over him.

The sound caught Setha's ear and she turned from the stove. A ready smile curved her mouth before she caught herself as if realizing she was giving away too much of her emotion.

"Hungry?" she asked, casting a speculative eye about her kitchen. "I sure hope you're hungry."

"Starved." He gave her a playful frown. "This about nerves again?"

She laughed. "No, it's not about nerves. Promise."

"Regrets?" he probed, tilting his head to one side.

"No." Her wide, onyx-colored eyes sparkled briefly before she looked away. "But…"

Khouri waited.

She went to grab a dish towel and wiped her hands. "It's just I—I don't want you to think this is the way I do business."

He shortened the distance between them then. "Hey?" He pulled the towel from her fingers and tossed it to the dish rack. "I hope it is. You'd be the best damn business meeting I've ever had. Bet on that."

"Khouri…" Her cheeks heated. She had hoped for a little more seriousness on his part.

He sobered a bit, cornering her in the angle at the stove and the counter. "Are you tryin' to tell me you won't sleep with me again?"

Cheeks positively burning then, Setha turned her face away. "We didn't sleep."

He put his hands on her, brushing his fingers against her thighs when he tugged the hem of his shirt she wore. "No, we didn't exactly sleep, did we?"

"We've got business, Khouri…."

"Would you like to have sex again, Setha?"

"Yes." The word sounded closer to a moan that was silenced when his mouth fell upon hers.

She didn't need to be coaxed into a response. Eagerly, she splayed her fingers across the enviable expanse of his defined torso. Her nails curved into his pecs when she stood on her toes and deepened the pressure of her tongue in his mouth. His hands delved beneath the shirt. Simultaneously, he squeezed her bottom while caressing her sex.

"Khouri…do more," she pleaded when she felt him barely spread her and *barely* ease a fingertip inside her. "Take me back to bed." The words sounded close to a purr.

He chuckled amid the kiss. "What's wrong with the counter?"

Setha's laughter ended on a gasp when he deepened

the caress and made love to her with more fingers. She didn't care where they were as long as he didn't stop.

Khouri used his free hand to probe into the shirt and help himself to the suppleness of her breasts. He kissed his way down the line of her neck, stopping briefly to nibble the satiny flesh at her collarbone. Both hands cupping her breasts, he hid his face in the molasses-dark valley between them and inhaled. Setha bit her lip, captivated by his gorgeous profile when he angled his head to suckle a nipple.

Sensation ran wild in the kitchen. Khouri was seconds away from freeing himself, when the phone rang… and kept ringing. The machine answered after four rings, but the caller was clearly set on speaking with the mistress of the house.

Khouri had Setha perched neatly atop the counter. The ringing of the phone once again persisted, however, sending tension down like an anvil. Instinctively, Khouri knew Setha's trembling had nothing to do with him…but her unease at over who the caller may have been.

"To hell with this," he muttered and went to snatch the receiver from its mount near the refrigerator.

Setha watched, her expression a cross between amazement and disbelief.

"Yeah?" The greeting came off as harsh as the look shadowing his appealing features. "Yes. No—no, you have the right number. Good morning."

Setha blinked, uncertainty creeping into her expression when his voice softened.

"Ms. Melendez is busy just now, could I take a message? Mmm-hmm…sure I'll remind her—no problem. Good morning to you, too." He replaced the phone.

"That was Valerie," he announced coolly, referring to Setha's assistant. "She doesn't want you to forget to sign off on the requisitions for the center."

Obviously relieved by the caller's identity, she made a mental note to handle the requisitions first thing. Her curiosity kicked in when she tuned in to Khouri on the phone again. It sounded as if he was speaking to friends that time. Friends who owned a security firm.

"Khouri?" she whispered, wriggling down off the counter while fixing his shirt she wore.

In no mood to listen, Khouri simply turned his back while making arrangements for a consultation to obtain a quote and set dates for a security system installation.

"...right, but we're headed out of town day after tomorrow...Mmm-hmm...Right...All right, sounds good. Thanks." Once again, Khouri replaced the receiver. That time, he received a slap to his shoulder and turned to face Setha's frown.

"You had no right to do that."

"No right at all, Ms. Melendez?" he challenged, taking her wrist in one hand while the other disappeared beneath the hem of the shirt. "Hmm?" he inquired, watching as her lashes fluttered in response to his probing fingers.

"This is my home," she managed to say. Barely. "I make the decisions."

"Trouble is, you're not makin' any to protect yourself, sugar."

All the while, he caressed her intimately. Setha couldn't stifle her response. "I don't want my family to know," she moaned.

Temper heating, Khouri forgot his arousal. "You

didn't see the way you just shut down when that damn phone started to ring."

"I was just caught off guard is all," she argued though she was rattled by the sound of his voice. "Hasn't that ever happened to you?"

"Not like that."

"Right." She pushed at his chest. "Don't big strong men get startled from time to time or is that emotion reserved for us little ole gals?"

"Stop." He leaned against the refrigerator and eased his hands into his trouser pockets. "Stop tryin' to make it out to be about that. I'm not one of your brothers. You won't pull me off topic by getting me all riled up about bein' a chauvinist."

Setha blinked and couldn't ignore the shiver that danced up her spine. He figured that quickly—too quickly. It was her preferred manner of getting out of uncomfortable talks with her family. She was usually out of the vicinity by the time they'd figured out what she'd done.

"It *is* about that, Khouri. It's *always* about that—always about strength and who has it. Men don't think women have enough to fill a thimble."

"Christ, Seth, is that what you think?"

She pressed her lips together, anger slowly fading from hearing her name shortened on his tongue.

Khouri was too heated to pay attention to her reaction. He rubbed all ten fingers through the cropped riot of curls atop his head and pushed off the refrigerator.

"Why can't this just be about me being scared that some idiot out there might be tryin' to kill you?" He shook his head, bright eyes locked and unwavering on her. "I'll do what I have to in order to prevent that."

Setha began to shake her head then, too. "Why? You—you barely know me."

"Hmph." He pinched the bridge of his nose. "One reason is because it's the right thing to do." He looked at her then. "The other is *because* I barely know you. I damn well intend to have a chance to. So could you please stop tryin' to be a Billie Badass and let me help you?"

Blinking and nodding, she made her silent promise to him.

Khouri turned on his heel and headed for the kitchen entryway. "I like my toast dry," he said over his shoulder.

"I didn't make any toast." Her voice sounded small.

He kept walking. "You better get to it then."

"Where are you going?" She was smiling then.

"To get one of my cards. It'll have all my numbers on it." He stopped to look back at her. "Email, snail address, you can even hit me up on Facebook or tweet me if that floats your boat." He made a move to turn.

"Khouri?" She waited for him to look her way again. "Thank you."

He smirked, took the time to graze her body hidden beneath his shirt and then pivoted about. "Finish my breakfast," he called.

Avra was finishing up her breakfast at The Archway, a local eatery not far from *Ross Review*. She'd hardly picked at her food, more interested in picking through the notes she'd been collecting on the evolving story behind Wade Cornelius's death. No one spoke on it during the funeral but the news was out that the man most certainly did *not* die of natural causes. He'd been stabbed once, but the cut nicked an artery. He had bled out slowly while trying to make his way from the secluded home he kept across town to get help.

Why would someone want him dead? Avra chewed the edge of a fork handle. Every instinct told her it all had to do with a story. Could that story have been about Melendez?

Then there was the news she'd received from David and Noah the night before. The research had turned up another very interesting link.

"Eating alone? Unsurprising."

Avra grimaced when the familiar rough baritone touched her ears. "Seeing as how we've got no business to discuss—thank God—there's no need to be civil." She kept her eyes downcast.

"May I join you?" Samson asked. "I'm sure you're not expecting anyone."

She gave him a phony smile. "Table's all yours. I was just leaving."

"Be a pal, Avra. Stay a little longer and trade barbs with me."

"Mornin', Mr. M."

Samson's dark eyes shifted slowly off Avra and he grinned at the young man who'd approached the table. "What's goin' on, Jared?"

"Get you a drink, Mr. M?"

"Just coffee." Sam turned back to Avra then. "Black—no sugar." He watched her until she met his gaze. "Ms. Ross'll have another—she takes just a trace of cream in hers...right, Av?"

Were she stronger, she could've bent the fork handle in half. She was just that tense if her clenched jaw was any indication.

"That'll be fine, Jared," she told the young waiter.

"See?" Sam's grin broadened in a roguish way. "Isn't this nice?" He unbuttoned the champagne-colored suit coat and settled his big frame into a chair.

"Did you know all the Melendez murder victims shared the same address?" she asked, eager to wipe the satisfaction from his all-too-gorgeous face. Her plan succeeded.

"How'd you—?"

"Oh, surely you didn't think this was a dead-end story?" she cut into his question, leaning across the table to study him with exaggerated curiosity. "We've had people on this since the first victim turned up."

Samson took a minute to scan the semicrowded restaurant dining room. "Could be a waste of time following up on that, you know?"

"Why? Because *Ross* only writes fluff for Melendez? I wonder why that is?"

"It's your paper." He waved a hand. "Maybe you should have a talk with your father." His eyes flashed with sudden intrigue. "What'd you mean about all the victims sharing the same address?"

"Just that." Avra relaxed in her chair. "Their work applications at MM all show the same address. At one time or another, anyway."

"How could you know that if it's—?"

"What? Confidential?" She let out an abrupt, humorless laugh and tugged the lace cuff of her navy blouse. "Sam, Sam...I know the good ole boy world is alive and kickin' in your neck of the woods, but this *is* the electronic age. This wasn't all that hard to dig up. Only question now is—where is it?" She stabbed a page with the fork she held. "The address doesn't turn up on any map or GPS locator—interesting, huh? Maybe you should be having a talk with *your* father, to?"

Jared returned with the coffees then.

"Put mine in a to-go cup, hon." Avra gathered her things. "Mr. M will be dining alone."

"All this contact information just for me? I hope I won't make anyone jealous," Setha teased.

Khouri smiled but continued making the cut into a portion of juicy beef sausage. "I'm a lone wolf, Seth—my love life is a sad story."

"But certainly not a lonely one."

Intrigued, Khouri brought his luminous gaze to her face. "You've asked about me?"

Setha barely shrugged. "Wasn't hard to do—especially when my mostly female staff heard I was meeting with you. I swear I never had so many offers for help." She reached for her mug and held it poised inches from her mouth. "I believe the term 'heartbreaker' was tossed about a time or two."

Khouri's playful wince was followed by a soft chuckling. "Lies," he swore while focusing on the folder of notes she'd collected.

"Hmph." Setha finished her coffee and then left the table to prepare a second helping of the sausage and egg breakfast.

"Seth?"

"Yeah?" She didn't turn away from covering the biscuits.

"Look at this."

Setha finished at the counter and then rounded the small kitchen table to peer over Khouri's shoulder. He held the John Holloway obit and read from it while she looked on.

"…survived by his wife, Vita, and two sons, Shane and Carson."

Dazedly, Setha backed away and slowly reclaimed her place at the table. "Could be coincidence," she breathed.

"Could be." He stroked his jaw. "Carson's not a very common name, though."

"No, not very." Setha held her head in her hands and groaned.

Chapter 12

Setha was smiling and on the verge of a full-blown grin. The credit for her easy mood went to the stack of glossies she'd pulled from the main group of possible photos. Not all the pictures were lurid depictions of women as sex objects. Some were quite good—artistic even.

She smirked, brushing her fingers across a picture that held a Western motif. She liked it in spite of the fact that the woman was dressed in chaps and not much else. She leaned against the hood of a well-maintained but dusty early model Lincoln Continental that was parked in front of a saloon.

Unfortunately, the shot couldn't keep her preoccupied forever. She set it aside and then buried her face in her hands as memory surged. Carson Arroyo is Carson Holloway?

At least she knew this wasn't all about her. Some

psycho hadn't singled her out for some sick reason. While the circumstances were still grim, the knowledge of that was somewhat comforting. But could she tell her family? She knew Khouri wanted that and she was no fool. She'd love to share it with them but knew they would just as soon hunt down Carson Arroyo and kill him as to look at him.

There was reason behind this. The man wasn't just some mindless creep out to hurt whoever crossed his path. Sadly, he didn't possess all the necessary skills to articulate his issues. Moreover, the need for vengeance had overruled all other sensible thought. She couldn't bring her family in on this—not yet. She needed to know if he was just lashing out at his father's employer because the man had worked too hard. Had Carson lashed out at Wade Cornelius for perpetuating a story that made his father look like a broke man who saw suicide as his only way out? Or had his father's employer played more of a role in contributing to the man's death? Had Wade Cornelius reported on a suicide that really wasn't?

Sam grimaced at the sound of the phone vibrating on the end table next to the chair he occupied in his den.

"Call you later, Pow," he said, having checked the faceplate and finding his brother's name there. He turned the phone off completely, tossed it aside and indulged in another swallow of bourbon while studying the mural on the opposite wall.

The piece was actually a replica from an old photo of his dad and friends. The painting never failed to relax Sam. The promise and excitement on his dad's young

face, when he was in the early days of his success, instilled both happiness and pride.

Samson's study of the portrait dimmed some of the
easiness illuminating his face then. He couldn't help
but think of all that his dad had to endure on his quest
for success. Sam had always drawn strength from the
knowledge of that fact.

Now, the man who gave him his strength was giving him cause for concern. He hadn't been able to get
Avra Ross off his mind since the day before.

She's always on your mind, a voice told him and
he promptly—silently—told it to shut up. This time,
it wasn't the woman herself but the news she'd shared.
The fact that the murder victims had all shared the same
address was too eerie to be coincidence. Still, that didn't
concern him half as much as the fact that the address
couldn't be located.

Groaning, Sam drained his glass and then let his
head fall back on the chair.

"Thank you, Avra." Avra's sarcastic stab at polite-
ness was directed toward her brother when she'd hunted
down the chopsticks and passed them his way.

"Are you sure it can't be found?" Khouri asked. He'd
been preoccupied for most of the lunch. He and Avra
shared Chinese takeout while she told him about the
address mystery and its connection to the Melendez
workers.

Shaking her head, Avra spoke around a mouthful
of lo mein. "Even checked it myself… Couldn't find a
damn thing." She swallowed. "Now why do you think
they'd lie about an address?"

"Maybe somebody told 'em to." Khouri drew tea

through a straw until only ice remained in the cup he held.

"Told to?"

"Come on, Av. It's no secret that Dan Melendez doesn't play by the rules. Who's to say that all or most of his employees are here illegally?"

Avra picked through the carton of noodles. "You think he'd exploit his own people that way?"

"When'd you get so naive? Hell, he wouldn't be the first." Khouri laughed.

"Anyway—" Avra threw up a flip wave "—this is the father of the woman you're in love with, remember?"

Khouri almost choked on the mound of sesame chicken he'd scooped into his mouth.

"Don't try to deny it." Avra selected a plump morsel of shrimp and savored the taste. "She's a knockout."

"You really think I'm that shallow?" He rocked his desk chair back and forth. "To fall for a woman because she looks good?"

"Yep," she replied without hesitation. "But it might be about more than that this time. I think you're intrigued more with her."

"Some kind of hero complex, or somethin'?"

"Well, given the way you met her, that'd make sense but it's not the reason, either."

"Hell, Av." Khouri ran his palm across his jaw. "Are you just in the mood for confusin' the devil out of me today?"

"Hmph." Avra's dark face was a picture of confidence. "You're intrigued because with all the danger this girl is in the midst of, she's not hiding behind her three big brothers and waiting like some helpless damsel for them to figure it all out and save her. She's gonna be involved and cut down anybody who tries to stand in her way." She stood to plop the half-empty lo mein container into the bag the takeout had arrived in.

"Face it, Khouri, the only 'difficult' women you've had to deal with have been the three of us." Avra referred then to herself and younger sisters Raquel and Fiona. "You've made it a point in your life to surround yourself with dimwits who've been happy to let the gorgeous, know-it-all Khouri Ross have his way."

She propped a slender hip to the bar where she'd eaten her lunch. "You never saw Miss Melendez comin' and she's got you turned around like a dog chasin' its tail."

Khouri rolled his eyes and helped himself to more of the chicken and sautéed vegetables he'd ordered.

"Well?" Avra spread her hands anticipating some form of a compliment. "Am I right?"

"No. She's stupid not to involve her brothers in this."

Smiling then, Avra wondered if her brother realized he had no argument save that one. *Poor thing,* she thought.

"You know she'd never forgive you if you brought them in on this behind her back?"

Khouri accepted his sister's warning with a gruff snort. "I know that."

"And she's not dumb for wanting to be a part of this. I can understand where she's comin' from."

"Hmph." Khouri leaned back to roll his sleeves a bit higher above his forearms. "I know that, too—it's exactly the type of dumb crap you'd try to pull. Correction—you *have* pulled it."

"My point exactly." She slapped the corner of the

shellacked bar top. "One overprotective brother—older *or* younger—can be hell on earth and that poor girl's had to deal with three of 'em all her life. Cut her some slack for bein' smart and independent, will you?"

Khouri muttered his next obscenity in a softer octave. "As usual you equate independence and intelligence with strength and invincibility."

"Ah…strength and invincibility—those impressive traits that men possess exclusively, huh?"

"I don't know why I bother talkin' to you." He wolfed down the rest of his meal.

"You talk to me 'cause every now and then you need to be told how foolish you're bein'."

Khouri didn't try to suppress his laughter over the comment. Avra joined in soon after.

Martino Viejo smiled as he often did while preparing for another day of work. Just stepping into his closet alone was enough to instill the deepest sense of happiness. He came into the United States wearing the clothes on his back with nothing in his pocket save a card that held the address to his salvation.

At least, that's what he thought it was and it had been…eventually.

Martino shook his head, sending sleek tendrils of black into his eyes. Now was not the time for a trip down that particular lane of his memory. He knew, though, that such things could not be avoided especially since the killings began.

He wouldn't buy into the fact that there were too many coincidences—too many things he had in common with the other victims. Could it mean nothing?

Or could it mean everything? So far, he hadn't been questioned or approached about any sort of protection.

He smirked. Protection? For him? Sure, he'd come a long way and was finally beginning to make a name for himself at Melendez. He certainly hadn't garnered any status that would merit him *protection* from the monster who was not only targeting U.S. emigrants, but U.S. emigrants who worked for Melendez—emigrants who had also been specially selected for other reasons.

Losing focus again, Martino left off selecting his outfit for the next day. He ventured deeper into his closet, where he retrieved a shoe box from the farther-most corner of the area. Removing the cover, he slowly fingered the contents of the box—memories of his ear-liest days in the States. They were days that, as yet, weren't tucked far enough away into the recesses of his memory.

Perhaps that wasn't such a bad thing. He recalled the phrase "never forget where you came from" *else you could wind up back there*. He always tacked that on. The remnants of that box were his way of never forgetting.

Wiping the back of his hands across suddenly moist eyes, Martino shoved the box back into the closet and returned to choosing his suit for the next day.

Khouri arrived at Setha's early that morning to find her home once again occupied by men. At least, this was a group he knew. Parking his truck, he crossed the front lawn and approached the head of Fillmore Securities.

"What's goin' on, RJ?" he called.

Rafe Fillmore, Jr. greeted his old friend with a hand-shake and hug. "What's up, buddy?"

"Getting an early start, huh?" Khouri noted, observing members of the Fillmore team at various places along the front of the house as they made notes regarding security concerns and solutions.

Rafe tugged the cap—emblazoned with his company's logo—off his head and scratched at his receding hairline. "Earlier the better. I know better than to play with a Texas sun in the middle of the day."

"I hear ya." Khouri chuckled and squinted up at the sky from behind his sunglasses. "So where's the lady of the house?"

"Man…" Rafe seemed to cringe. "That's one angry lil gal. I'd rather be in a scuffle with one of her brothers than her."

Khouri's chuckles deepened. "Guess she's not too happy about y'all being here."

"That's puttin' it way too mild, K, my man."

Khouri eased his keys into a side pocket on his carpenter's jeans and looked around the yard. "Where is she?"

"Off fussin' with her pistols." Rafe appeared to shudder.

Laughing fully then, Khouri clapped RJ's back and went to look for Setha. He found her far off across the massive expanse of her back lawn. She'd put away her pistols and was then firing a double-barreled shotgun at what looked to be a row of cans set along a wooden fence which stood at an impressive distance.

Smiling, he strolled toward her. He could easily figure what she was angry about. For a second, he reconsidered walking up to her. His thoughts carried him back to what Avra had said about his usual taste in women.

While he hadn't exactly sought her out, he knew he would have, based on her looks alone. But what of the rest? He'd had her sexually several times and in varied positions since they had met. He could walk away. She was already pissed with him. They were on a good track with the ad campaign—others could take over from there. He knew none of that would make a difference though. The woman had him completely and thoroughly wrapped around her fingers. What's more, he knew she did. While he'd do everything he could to maintain some aspects of control, he knew he didn't mind it a bit.

Khouri whistled just as she let off another shot. It missed the cans. In fact, it looked as though she had yet to knock one from the fence.

"RJ said you were one angry lil gal," he teased.

Setha's smile was grim. "I'm just likin' that man more 'n' more." She let off another shot.

Khouri leaned down a little to speak directly into her ear. "Is it my face you're seeing on those cans?"

"Hmm…" Another thunderous shot ran out from the gun and hit a can dead center. "Thanks for the tip."

Khouri smiled and shook his head. "Sugar, can't you understand this is all for—"

"My own protection. Got it." She hit another can. "Get your hand off my ass," she grumbled at his touch.

He adored her stubbornness but didn't remove his hand. "I can think of you tellin' me it was mine more than once."

Lashes fluttering, Setha tightened her grip on the gun. "Funny, isn't it? The idiotic things that come out of a woman's mouth when somethin's goin' on between her legs."

Khouri only moved in closer. His fingers disappeared beneath the frayed hem of the denim cutoffs she wore with a wash-worn short-waist blouse. Squeezing a bare cheek, he nuzzled her ear. "I hope you enjoyed what was going on then?"

Calmly, Setha replaced her gun in its casing and secured the lock. She sent Khouri a scathing look and then stomped off.

Still encouraged, Khouri pulled off his sunglasses and watched her. "Yep, that's one angry lil gal."

Chapter 13

Setha's mind was set on getting to her bedroom where she planned to spend the rest of the day—or at least until Khouri and that blasted security team were gone. She rolled her eyes while moving with purpose up the stairway.

She cursed herself for acting like a spoiled princess or, as RJ had so aptly labeled her, an "angry lil gal." Despite the fact that he'd grown up around three women, Khouri still didn't get it. Her home was the one place where *she* called the shots. Her father and her brothers' opinions took a backseat to what *she* thought was best.

The fact that Khouri Ross had waltzed in and rearranged things to his satisfaction wasn't what frustrated her most. Knowing she'd let him do it, with little-to-no argument, was the stinger.

"Dammit," she whispered, feeling the dull throb of arousal over the memory of his hands on her body.

She remembered the deep, sweet octave of his voice so close to her ear....

"Get your mind out of your panties, Setha..." She pushed open the bedroom door and felt her upper arm being gripped shortly after.

"Please don't do that," Khouri urged while escorting her inside the room. His mouth was on hers before the door shut with her pressed against it.

Setha was a happy participant, smoothing her hands up and across the broad plane of his chest. Then, she remembered that she was angry with him.

Ignoring the subtle shoves to his torso, Khouri expertly unfastened her shorts and insinuated his hand down in front. He broke the kiss when he realized she wasn't wearing anything beneath the denim cutoffs.

"Stop... I'm mad at you," she moaned and then moaned again when his fingers were inside her and thrusting high.

She gasped in the midst of battling his tongue with her own. "I have a houseful of people."

Khouri hooked his free hand about her thigh and tugged, increasing the play space for his lunging and rotating fingers. "I guess you better keep your voice down." The advice came seconds before his tongue eased past her lips again.

To hell with it. Setha gave in to what she wanted. Languidly, she moved in response to his thrusts and wavering cries escaped her throat.

Boldly, she moved in to undo the loose-fitting carpenter's jeans, but he stopped her before she could unzip him. He wanted more time to play, knowing once he was out of his pants, the only place he'd want to be was inside her.

He continued to fondle her intimately, but let go of her thigh preferring to cup her breast beneath the wrinkled lilac blouse. Setha went back to undoing his pants only to have her hands slapped. She happily settled for raking her nails over the muscular forearms that were visible thanks to the short-sleeved shirt he wore. Her hands went weak though, once her shorts were gone, her blouse was undone and his hands covered her bare breasts. She hadn't even felt him take off her bra.

Awkwardly, she moved against the dual caress he plied to her neck and collarbone. "Khouri…" She tugged his waistband insistently.

"But you've got a houseful of—"

"Shut up." Setha moved from the door, forcing him back while she nudged his chest with hers. At her bed, she wasted no time pushing him down to the center and then went about the task of relieving him of his shirt.

Khouri let her have her way and felt his heart stop in his chest when she looked at him. Emotion stirred deep and devastating.

"I don't feel comfortable doing this," he teased to dispel the emotion and the questions it roused.

Setha grinned, her wavy locks framing her dark face like a storm cloud. Grinning more devilishly, she freed the erection straining behind his button fly. She bit her lip in a naughty manner while her nails grazed every rigid caramel-covered inch of his sex.

"You'll survive," she promised and then began her assault, dropping soft kisses down his beautifully cut torso moving with devastating purpose below his waist.

"But I don't think you'll last very long," she predicted at the sound of his sharp intake of breath when she stroked him with her tongue.

Khouri savored the caress, wanting as much as she elected to give. He knew what she said was right— he wouldn't survive long if he indulged as he wanted. Reasserting his strength, he drew her up to kiss him deeply.

Setha nudged her bare sex against his until she felt the rough edges of the condom packet he'd pressed into her palm. A split second after she had it in place, he took her waist and settled her beautifully. Again, Setha bit her lip while winding and raising herself along his very appealing endowment. She luxuriated in the sensation of his hands roaming over every part of her.

"Hush up…" Khouri ordered when her pleasure affected the volume of her cries.

Setha bit down on her lip yet again. Her eyes were shut tight and she moaned without shame while working herself up and down his shaft as she introduced him to his own special place inside her.

Khouri studied every change in her expression as she took him rigorously. He couldn't help but be affected by the ecstasy claiming her lovely face. His own satisfaction heightened then sharply and he clutched her arching hips a tad tighter.

Setha didn't collapse onto him until sometime after. She released and clenched him inside her walls until the groans he uttered were a cross between pleasure and pain. She melted, dropping lazy kisses to his pecs as they flexed beneath her lips.

Located along the Texas Coastal Bend on Galveston Bay, the city of Kemah was home to an elaborate boardwalk hailed for fine restaurants, shops and hotels. Named for the Indian word meaning "wind in my face," the area possessed an elegant beauty like no other. Having a breathtaking view overlooking the bay didn't hurt things, either.

Setha stood motionless after being escorted from the chopper on the small, private airstrip that had carried her and Khouri on the brief trek from Houston to Galveston.

Khouri finished his conversation with the pilot and came to take Setha to the waiting Infiniti Crossover. Setha fell in step but Khouri kept her from getting into the car when they approached.

"I'm sorry," he said and smiled at the stunned look that crept into her vivid dark eyes. "I had no right to bully you about the security but you didn't see what I saw the night you came barreling into me behind Rocky's club." He shook his head, toying with her braided ponytail. "You were terrified. Call it chauvinistic but I'm not used to *not* being able to help a woman in distress."

"But you *did* help." She smoothed her hands across his cheeks. She could feel the muscles flex near his jaw.

"Right." He rolled his eyes. "Dialing 9–1–1 and letting you hide in my car. Big whoop."

She curled her fingers into the neckline of his black polo shirt. "It was enough, trust me."

"Will you let me finish?"

Setha folded her arms and waited.

Khouri followed her example, folding his arms over his chest. He spared a moment to observe the black Jordans peeking out from the hem of his jeans. "I'm not trying to stifle who you are, Seth." He started to massage a bicep, and then changed his mind and reached for her hand instead.

"I'm not tryin' to bulldoze you into going my way, either." He focused on rubbing his thumbs across her knuckles. "I know you had enough of that growing up...."

Setha followed his every move. She wasn't about to interrupt, especially when it seemed he was uneasy about speaking his mind.

Khouri must have sensed that he'd said too much for he cut himself off. Pressing his lips together, he grimaced over whatever he'd been about to say. "Just tell me when I'm goin' overboard, all right?"

She eyed him skeptically. "You're sure?"

He at first replied with a smirk. "Don't mean you'll change my mind," he warned.

"You still might regret saying it."

"We'll see." He opened the passenger door and waved her into the car.

Setha tried not to express disappointment when she discovered Khouri had arranged for separate rooms at the inn. They weren't even adjoining. She wouldn't overthink what he had said at the airstrip largely because she thought he was about to tell her that he loved her.

Was he ready to say that? Was she ready to hear it?

A knock at the door finished the thought. Setha moved past the case she was unpacking and sprinted for the door. There, she found the answer to her question.

Yes. She was definitely ready to hear it. She didn't realize how deeply she smiled while watching him lean against the doorjamb and looking oh so adorable while he did it.

"Up for dinner?" he asked, a hint of uncertainty dwelling in his bright gaze. "Or would you rather stay in?"

Staying in would be her first choice, but she was determined to relax. "I'd love to go out." She almost burst into laughter at the shock on his face.

After all, this was about business, right? She couldn't let Carson Arroyo or Holloway or whatever the hell his name was, dictate her moves forever, could she?

"Maybe we can get some more ideas for the campaign."

"Right." The tone of his voice clearly relayed that the idea held little interest for him. "You ready?"

Setha patted her khaki capris in search for her room key. She grabbed her purse from the message desk. "Let's do this."

"So what do you think?" Khouri twisted his Heineken bottle on the wooden table and watched Setha bumping the mouth of her wineglass to her lips.

She seemed in awe of Kemah's late-evening skies though she'd seen them many times before. They sat in the patio dining area of a seafood eatery not far from the inn.

"I think we should shoot the entire campaign from here," she said as though she were dazed.

Khouri laughed, turning his stare toward the sunset. A row of palms, at varying heights, lined the beach where the water hit the surf in soft shades of oranges, reds and golds. The water itself was a vivid purplish blue that didn't seem real.

"You think we can get Samson and Av to go for this?"

Setha sipped at the fragrant sauvignon blanc. "I believe we can get 'em to go along with it." She closed her eyes and savored the taste of the treat on her tongue and the breeze in her face. "I think they're both ready to put it to bed."

Khouri's laughter was louder then and seemed to vibrate in the night air.

"What?" Setha asked, delighted shivers coursing through her at the sound of his laughter.

"Nothing. I agree with you." He shrugged and reached for his beer. "I think they're both ready to... put it to bed."

Setha was next to fall into laughter and they enjoyed the amusement at their siblings' expenses.

She noticed him staring, the bottle poised at his mouth. "Sorry." She cleared her throat on her laughter. "My family's got some pretty wild laughs."

"I like it." He tossed back a swig. "I can tell you like doing it. I'd be very upset if you stopped."

Humor fading, Setha topped her nails to the stem of the glass. "Hasn't been much to laugh about lately."

Khouri reached for her hand and toyed with her fingers. "Guess we're gonna have to change that, right?"

She squeezed his hand. "You're already my protector—can't expect you to be my comedy board, as well." She tilted her head when he frowned. "What? Did I say something wrong?"

"My sisters always call me that." He tugged his earlobe and smirked. "They don't mean it as a compliment."

"Ah..." Setha studied the swaying palm leaves against the breeze and considered her reply. "Little sisters don't like to be policed—I can tell you that."

"Hmph. Boy, didn't I learn *that* the hard way."

Setha settled back in her chair and observed the man across from her. Silently, she noted what a job it must've been to wrangle three rowdy sisters. That experience had most likely laid the foundation for his coolly serious demeanor—a facet to his personality which only added to the mystique itself.

"Well, if it helps," she said as she gave a saucy toss of her head and decided to put a teasing spin on the moment, "I think all your…dealings with your sisters are one of the things that make you so successful with women."

Khouri blinked and studied her with renewed interest. The waitress returned to the table to ask about appetizers.

"So how do you know I'm successful?" he asked once the server had left with the order.

Setha felt her lips part in surprise. *Did the man even own a mirror?* she wondered.

"I asked about you," she admitted, fiddling with the long lacy cuff of her blouse. "I couldn't help but ask given my entire female staff kept asking if you would be taking any meetings in *our* office.

"But they did tell me you're something of a heartbreaker," she added once the laughter softened between them.

"Yeah." He nodded slowly. "I can see why they'd say that. My relationship record isn't the best."

"Why is that?" Setha asked, sipping her wine.

"I lose interest. Quick."

"Mmm…more quickly than they do?"

"Usually."

"And do you know why?"

"Avra thinks I'm not being challenged." Khouri pinched the bridge of his nose. "With every woman in my family bein' freakishly headstrong."

Setha erupted into more laughter.

"She says I choose…*softer*-tempered women in my love life, but lose interest because they're not what I truly want."

"Is she right?"

"I think she may have a point." Khouri's bright deep-set stare didn't waver from Setha's face.

The appetizers arrived and the couple spent several moments selecting potato skins and onion peels.

"So you said my *dealings* with women were only *one* of the things that make me so successful with women. Care to share more?"

Setha broke off a piece of one of the loaded skins. "It's gotta be your cologne, of course." She peeked at him through the fringe of her lashes. "What am I gonna have to do to get you to tell me what it is?"

"Ah, Miss Melendez." He wolfed down one of the potato skins and watched her smugly as he chewed. "That list would be long and varied and very X-rated."

Setha's robust laughter rose again.

Chapter 14

The next morning, Setha was on the phone with Samson. She was telling him her thoughts on using Kemah for all the shots. He thought it sounded like a fine idea and was well aware of the area and its beauty.

"I still want you to take a trip down and see the spots we have in mind for this thing, Sam."

"Hell, Set, I trust you. I'm just glad you took the reins on this thing and got some results."

"I'm no ad person, Sam. That's why Khouri and I want you and Avra here to take a closer look—"

"Ugg…" Sam's deep voice sounded close to a growl.

"Sam?"

"Fine, fine. So long as we come down there at separate times."

Setha laughed.

"I'm serious."

"I gotta go." The bell was chiming at her room door.

"Setha, you know I mean that."

"Bye, Sam," she sang into the phone before clicking it off. She was still laughing when she opened the door to Khouri.

He'd barely passed the doorway when his hand cuffed her neck and he was kissing her slow and deep.

Setha could feel her earlier amusement shift into something intense and desperate. Restlessly, she raised a bare thigh along the side of his rough denims. Khouri lifted her, kicking the door shut and carrying her to the unmade bed. She was out of the simple pink nightshirt in an instant. His big hands roamed her flawless molasses-dark skin, causing her to shiver and feel even more desperate for his touch.

"Khouri..."

He curled a fist against the small of her back and told himself not to get carried away. "I came to ask you about breakfast." He gnawed the soft flesh of her shoulder and squeezed her buttocks relentlessly.

Setha curved her legs about his waist drawing him deeper into the tangled covers. "I love it," she purred, purposefully misunderstanding and trailing kisses down his neck and inside his shirt.

"I meant... Jesus..." He began to thrust against her, his erection straining for release. "I meant outside, Seth..."

"Mmm..." She met his mock thrusts passionately. "I prefer it inside..."

"Seth," he grunted and tugged her up to sit. "You'll get it," he promised.

"Now?" she taunted, lying back down and circling her hips in an intentionally naughty fashion. She giggled devilishly, playfully, her dark eyes sparkling as they roamed his face.

You've gone and done it, Khouri my man, he silently acknowledged and watched her then more intently than he realized. He'd gone and fallen in love with a woman he'd never seen coming. And he'd never been happier.

Setha took his expression to mean he was serious about breakfast. "Just give me twenty minutes, okay?" She scooted close and brushed a kiss across his jaw and then disappeared into the bathroom.

Khouri moved to the foot of the bed and covered his head with his hands. How had it happened?

Fool, he called himself. She was incredible. He'd been hooked almost from the moment he had met her. Did he dare tell her that? Would he scare her the way he was scaring himself?

The utter beauty and sun-kissed atmosphere of the boardwalk had Setha marveling again. She and Khouri strolled arm in arm in the midst of other couples, kids and vendors.

Khouri felt her hand tighten on his arm. He didn't need to ask what was wrong once he spied the set look on her dark face.

Setha blinked, and then shook her head and sent him a quick smile when she felt him staring.

"Don't even try it." He tugged her arm and drew her over to stand with him along the railing. "Did you see him?"

"No. I swear it." She tugged the hem of the throw-back Cowboys' jersey he wore. "I promise, Khouri."

He didn't look all that convinced, but drew her hand

threw the crook of his arm and continued their stroll. "When did you know he was following you?"

Setha leaned back her head while working to recall it. "Not long after he came to my office. I was last to leave one day and I saw a car just sitting…" She squeezed Khouri's bicep reassured by the unyielding muscle. "I wasn't sure it was him at first but I know that car wasn't empty."

"Son of a b…" Khouri murmured.

"There's the roller coaster," she pointed out. "And the Ferris wheel. Lord, that's a big one…."

"When did you know he wanted you dead?"

"Wasn't hard to figure out after that day." The question had drained her interest in the sights, as well. "Every time I looked up, he was there. He didn't do anything—not until that night at your sister's club."

"Son of a b." The phrase came through much louder that time.

"Look, a fragrance shop." Setha left Khouri's side and waltzed across the boardwalk before he could say anything.

"Mornin', miss!"

The proprietor of the shop was a darkly tanned, gregarious-looking man with a long salt-and-pepper beard and laughing green eyes. He greeted Setha with a double wave in addition to the words.

"Now what's a pretty lil thing like you in the market for?"

"Do you sell men's cologne?" Setha asked, a sly smile coming to the full curve of her mouth.

"Ah, miss! We have an extraordinary selection of fragrances for all the sexes!"

Setha cocked a brow. "All?"

"Why, yes. Male, female and undecided!"

She laughed. "Well, the cologne I'm looking for—a friend wears it and he wears it very well."

"And the name of the scent, ma'am?"

"Well…that's the problem. He won't tell me what it is."

"Well—" The man caught sight of Khouri before he could ask more. "Well, well…"

"What's goin' on, Jim," Khouri greeted the man with laughter and a hearty handshake. "Jim Beaumont, Ms. Setha Melendez." He made the introduction.

"This is where you got the cologne?" she asked Khouri after shaking hands with Jim. "Well, what's it called?" She shifted her gaze between the two men.

"It's not in my nature to refuse a beautiful woman, but I'd be taking my life in my own hands if I revealed that choice bit of info."

Khouri shook his head in response to Setha's inquisitive expression. "Jim means I've threatened to kill him if he ever tells the name of that cologne to anyone I know."

"Quite protective of his cologne, isn't he?" Setha sent a sideways glance toward Jim, who shrugged.

"Most of my clients wear one-of-a-kind fragrances which I create right here on these premises."

"Well, that's impressive." Setha propped her elbows to the countertop. "I'd love to talk with you more about that."

"Setha…" Khouri warned.

She waved him off. "I'm interested in having something made for myself." She pulled a card from her black quilted tote bag.

"Right." Khouri drew her close and extended his hand to shake with Jim.

"Stop by before you leave town." Jim winked. "You're a lucky man, Ross." He smiled approvingly at Setha.

Danilo Melendez looked up from the crop reports he was studying and smirked when his long-time associate Luke Anton walked into his office.

"Isn't it a little early to be frowning so, amigo?" Dan inquired.

Luke dropped a newspaper to the desk and waited. After a moment, he pointed to the story he'd come to discuss.

MURDER VICS MELENDEZ EMPLOYEES

"You know it's only a matter of time before other newspapers release this." Luke folded his arms over the vest he wore and watched Danilo scan the write-up. "Everyone's not as accommodating as Basil Ross," he added.

"Calm down, Luke—"

"I am calm." Luke pointed to the paper. "*Now,* however, is definitely the time for you to get out in front of this thing. Next, they'll be accusing us of killing our own workers to save money or some other trumped-up mess."

Dan pushed the paper to the side. "There's no reason for the police to suspect we're involved with murdering our own people. The mere idea of it is ludicrous."

"It would be were it not for certain skeletons in many of our closets, Dan."

Dan blinked, the words having stirred his attention. "You may leave before you say too much." He stood behind the desk.

"Get out in front of this, Dan."

"And say what?" Dan eased both hands into the pockets of his pin-striped trousers. "Exactly what will *getting out in front of it* accomplish?"

"It could save a lot of embarrassment should one of those skeletons start to speak."

"Are you threatening me, Luke?" Dan stood back on his long legs and regarded his associate with a cool, black stare.

Luke smiled. "And what would be the point in that?"

The men stared each other down for the better part of thirty seconds and then Luke stormed out of the office.

Dan was slow to return to his desk chair. Once he settled down, he reached for the phone and dialed out.

"Yes, Basil Ross, please."

"Thank you for seeing me," Avra said when she arrived to meet with Vita Arroyo that afternoon.

"I did not think it wise to turn down an interview from a Ross," the woman said, her melodious voice harboring a trace of curiosity.

"I'm sorry for what that story did to your family," Avra said once she stood in the middle of the woman's living room.

"You have nothing to apologize for." Vita wrapped her dusky-blue cardigan around a still-alluring figure-eight frame. "You were a child when all that happened. As for the story…it didn't do half as much damage as Melendez did when they fired my husband."

"But the reports, the story…" Avra began to fidget

with the gold bracelet peeking out from a tailored cuff of her shirt. "It said your husband killed himself because he was fired and couldn't support you all."

"Please," Vita urged Avra to have a seat.

"It's true, my husband was depressed." She braced elbows to knees and drew her fingers through a hoard of blue-black curls. "The financial problems after he lost his job were…massive but he did *not* kill himself."

"Did you tell the police?"

Vita's mouth curved on the threshold of a laugh. "Now that would have been a waste of everyone's time."

Avra scooted to the edge of the brown recliner. "Do you think Melendez was responsible for your husband's death?"

"Why are you involving yourself in this, child?"

"I don't want my father and everything he's worked for getting caught up in any Melendez crap." Avra shook her head and kept her gaze stony. "I think he's misplaced his loyalties all these years."

A thoughtful look came to Vita's light-brown face and her mouth curved once more. "I'm sure your father knew what he was doing, *bonita.* Anyway—" she sighed when Avra studied her strangely "—my biggest regret is how it affected my boys." Again, she dragged her fingers through her hair.

"I raised Shane and Carson under my maiden name after… It was easier that way."

"But still difficult?" Avra guessed.

Vita nodded, wrapping tighter into her sweater. "They had lived a wonderful life up until John was fired." She left the sofa and went to the mantelpiece that carried photos in frames of various sizes.

"Shane was older—always had a stronger mind. Car-

son… He never understood why things had to change."
She shook her head while studying the pictures. "His
entire mood changed. He hated being poor—he said it
all the time. Being poor while those responsible lived
well…it ate at him…changed him."

"Why was your husband fired?"

Vita looked around at Avra as if she'd forgotten she
wasn't alone. "I, um…have things to do, Ms. Ross, so
if you—"

"Was he at fault or—"

"I live very well, Ms. Ross—all that happened a
long time ago."

Avra left the chair. "But don't you want to know
why he was killed?"

"I do know and that's why it's a shame Wade Cornelius is dead." Vita's wide eyes snapped with unmis-
takable fire. "He could share all the facts that were
somehow omitted from his story." She headed for the
foyer and pulled open the door.

Avra grabbed her purse from the coffee table.
"Thank you for your time," she said on her way out.

After a day of sightseeing and scouting locales
across Kemah and Galveston, for good measure, Setha
and Khouri returned to the inn for a good dinner and
showers in their respective rooms.

Later, Setha stood outside in the hall calling herself
a desperate idiot.

"To hell with it," she muttered and applied a firm
knock to Khouri's door. He took a while to answer and
she would have lost her nerve had he not pulled open
the door just then. He didn't speak right away which
gave her the chance to start.

"I'm sorry. I know it's been a long day." She blinked uncontrollably and rubbed her hands incessantly. "I know we're both tired."

Surprised to find her outside his door, Khouri was still having trouble finding his voice. He simply moved aside so she could enter.

Wringing her hands, Setha suddenly had trouble finding her words, as well. Her present attire was probably saying enough, of course. She'd worn her pj's on the short trip to his room. Her smile was faint when she turned to find him still standing near the door.

"I thought we could talk a little if that's okay," she explained.

"I love you."

The simply spoken phrase rendered Setha frozen. She stood there until her legs demanded she sit.

"Oh," she said.

Khouri blinked, appearing as though he couldn't believe he'd said the words. Restlessly, he began to pace and rub his hands across his impressively sculpted abdomen.

"I thought I'd find a better way when it was time to say it."

"I love you, too," she cut into his ramble and smiled when his legs seemed to give out.

"Guess we're both masters of poor timing," she said when he leaned against the message desk just inside the room.

"Not so sure about that." His light eyes trailed her attire.

Setha waited a beat and then stood and simply unbuttoned her shirt. Wearing only the pajama bottoms, she walked toward him.

Khouri couldn't move from his leaning stance against the desk, but his stare spoke volumes. He whispered a hushed curse of approval moments before he raised his hands to cover the dark-chocolate-colored mounds bared to his gaze. Engaging her in a kiss, it was wet and throaty seconds later. Smoothly, he lifted her up to straddle his waist, then he returned to fondling the ample, bouncing orbs.

As his chest was already bare, Setha granted her hands free reign over the sleek caramel-colored plane. Accomplishing twin goals of torturing him and pleasuring herself, she nudged a nipple against his. The weak moan escaping his throat brought a smile to her face.

Khouri lifted her again; that time, to take her to his bed. He settled down to feast on her breasts once he'd dropped her to the center. He treated her breasts for only a few seconds and then moved on, working his way down her body. The pink-and-gray pajama bottoms contrasted sharply yet complementary against her flawless dark skin. Khouri tugged them over her hips and groaned when he saw that she was nude beneath.

"Damn, lady, don't you own any panties?" he muttered while his mouth skimmed her hip bone.

Setha giggled. "I promise to wear them the next time."

"Don't bother...."

Setha's giggling ended on a gasp when he nuzzled her thighs. From there, his lips blazed a trail toward what he craved. She bumped herself against his cheek, silently requesting more intimate attention.

Khouri didn't make her wait. Setha curled her fingers into the close silky crop of his hair and melted into the act. She raked her nails across the top of Khouri's head, urging him deeper. A disappointed whimper rumbled from her throat when he grabbed her wrists and moved above her.

Kisses rained down across her hips, tummy and chest. He turned her to her stomach and treated her back and shoulders to the same attention. Setha nuzzled her face into a pillow and arched her bottom when she felt him outlining that area of her anatomy with the tip of his nose.

He lifted her a bit higher and then, sliding both hands beneath to fondle and stroke her sex. Meanwhile, he subjected her to an oral treat from behind.

Setha's cries heightened during which she begged him not to stop. He did, of course, before she could climax. The respite was only to give him time to apply protection. He took her there from behind. Her cries became shaky moans and she was then pliant in his grasp.

Khouri accepted the challenge. He gnawed the back of Setha's neck while luxuriating in the feel of her silky locks between his fingers. Flexing them there, he encouraged her to rise.

Setha gripped the headboard, shuddering his name as they writhed against each other in thorough and mindless need.

"Mmm…no…." Khouri grunted, not ready for an end to the act when he felt the telltale signs of release. He would have withdrawn but Setha reached around clutching his thigh to keep him right where he was.

Helpless then himself, Khouri rested his head to her shoulder and submitted. Simultaneously he and Setha climaxed and then dropped to the covers and into sleep.

Chapter 15

"Are you serious?"

"Hey...I resent that."

"Houston?"

"Houston."

Setha shook her head while she and Khouri made the hike from the private plane to his SUV waiting across the tarmac. She couldn't have been more surprised when he announced that their next scouting locale for the Machine Melendez account would be right in their own backyards.

Of course, she couldn't find much fault in the decision. She'd have probably considered it herself once the excitement of the scouting trip began to wear out its welcome. Houston, Texas, definitely had more than its fair share of dazzling and sexy places from which to shoot the new advertising art.

"There're more great places to shoot from than my rooftop, you know?"

Khouri's voice merged into her thoughts like a rich syrup might course the bark of a tree—slow and provocative. Setha sent him a sideways glance and then bowed her head and nodded.

"That rooftop of yours is pretty hard to top, you know?" She grinned in spite of herself. "No pun intended," she added.

Khouri chortled while rooting around in a deep denim pocket for keys to the waiting Rover. "Yeah, it *is* pretty great," he drawled, his voice softer as he acknowledged the fact.

"Can I ask you something?" They were at the truck, but Setha turned and leaned against the passenger-side door before he could pull it open for her.

"Whatever you want," he obliged, reaching out to smooth away a lock of her hair from the corner of her eye.

She cleared her throat, but there was no sound. "On the roof...that day," she began once she discovered where her voice had run off to, "when I kissed you. Why didn't you kiss me back?" She tilted her head, closely observing him when he appeared to be taking his time producing an answer.

"Wanted you to act first," he admitted, weighing the keys in his palms and smirking over his response. "I, um...wasn't too sure about your status after that mess in the alley. When you *did* make the move, it threw me, I guess—that damn well never happened before." He leaned back on his long legs and waited on her reaction. "I'm sorry if I upset you," he tacked on when she kept her head down.

Setha began to shake her head then. "Wasn't that. I mean...it was. I—damn..."

"What?" He tugged on the hem of the burgundy tunic top she wore with denim capris.

Tossing back her head, she rolled her eyes and debated on whether to confess her thoughts. She acknowledged that what he'd just shared couldn't have been easy for him to admit. The least she could do was to be just as forthcoming.

"I guessed you were a man who wasn't used to a woman making the first move." Her heart lilted when his full, contagious laughter hit the air.

"Setha, Setha..." He moved close, dropping a kiss to her collarbone, exposed as a breeze beat against the material of her blouse. His mouth lingered there for a lengthy period and then with a ragged sigh, he stepped back. "You are definitely not looking at a man who takes issue to a woman making the first move. It tells me a lot."

"What does it tell you?" Her dark gaze was riveted on his bright one.

Again, Khouri was toying with her hair. "That you want what I'd like to give you."

Her lips had barely parted in reaction to his candor, when his mouth slanted across hers. The pressure was beckoning and coaxed her lips farther apart to welcome his tongue which barely circled and thrust against hers. He kissed her fully then. Setha eased her hands up along the rust-colored polo shirt that complemented his caramel-toned skin. She arched into his tall, athletic frame then, taking what he gave and giving in return.

* * *

"Are we going to your place?" Setha asked later. Khouri had bypassed her exit and he appeared to be heading downtown.

"Not quite," he said, risking a glance at his wrist-watch before smoothly maneuvering the Rover around the slower-moving vehicle in front of him. "We're gonna take a look at good ole Houston from a visitor's viewpoint."

"Come again?" Setha turned on the seat to watch him curiously.

"I booked rooms at the Seasons," he said as though that was nothing out of the ordinary.

Setha was watching him with a mix of humor and disbelief. "A little much?"

"How do you figure?"

Her humor and disbelief intensified. "That's a five-star hotel."

"Your point?" He handled the traffic with finesse while their verbal sparring match continued. "This is heavy business we're taking care of here."

"Exactly." Setha studied the Houston skyline coming into view. "It's business—a scouting trip meaning we're not even gonna get much use out of those five-star rooms."

"Not so, Miss M. I plan on getting every bit of my money's worth." He turned his head, giving her the benefit of his gaze shielded by the sunglasses he wore.

Setha didn't need to see his eyes to note the sugges-tion of his words. Their meaning reached out to caress every part of her. At that point, she didn't care where he took her so long as he made good on what his words promised.

"So, is the Seasons your usual spot to 'get your money's worth'?" She settled back against the seat while issuing the tease.

"It's my usual spot when I don't want to be found." His voice had taken on a hushed, thoughtful tone.

Setha turned her head on the butter-soft rest and regarded the outline of his striking profile. "Pretty hard to go incognito at a five-star spread, don't you think?"

"Ah, Miss M…" He angled the powerful SUV around another vehicle. "Only if you take the penthouse."

Ezekiel Jaiquez was about to leave his five-star property when Khouri and Setha arrived. The hotel entrepreneur remained behind the front desk to welcome the new guests and old friends.

"EJ." Khouri reached out to take the man's hand in a tight grip as they made a pretense at hugging across the desk.

"How's Fee?" EJ's tone was as intent as his stare while he waited for a response.

Grinning, Khouri shook his head at the man's usual inquiry. "Fiona's still too young for you," he issued his usual reply.

"Hell, man, how long you gonna give me grief?" EJ placed a hand across the Adidas logo in the corner of the T-shirt he sported for a casual visit to check up on one of his many businesses. "So I was ten when she was—"

"Four. Like I said, 'too young for you.'"

The men shared robust laughter until EJ noticed Setha who had been laughing as hard as the two of them.

"Well, damn, girl, long time no see."

"How you doin', EJ?" Setha stood on her toes to embrace him and accept his kiss to her cheek.

Khouri leaned against the tall, white oak desk and watched the exchange.

Setha noticed and waved a hand. "I've used EJ's other hotels for some of my fundraising events."

"I see." Khouri raised a brow in EJ's direction. "You know I'll have to tell Fee about this."

"Aw, man!" EJ threw back his head and clutched his heart. "Can't a brotha get a break?"

Laughter and boisterous conversation carried between the threesome for a long while.

"EJ's on a roll. I had no idea he owned this place, too."

"Don't tell me he hasn't tried to get you here a time or two?" Khouri asked, unable to help but be mildly curious about the particulars of Setha's relationship with the hotel connoisseur.

Setha frowned, genuinely confused. "No…he actually never mentioned this place for an event."

Khouri had to laugh. "I don't think he would've had the place in mind for charity, Seth."

Her steps slowed during their walk from the elevator bay to their rooms. "Well what, then?"

"Enough," Khouri ordered in a teasing tone, barely able to maintain his steps behind the porter who carried their bags. "I refuse to believe you're *this* clueless about your looks."

"What?" Setha almost stopped her steps then, too.

Khouri only turned to her, arms spread in silent explanation.

She rolled her eyes in understanding. "Honey, I grew

up with three brothers and those jokers never let me get too full of myself."

The porter had opened one of the main doors to the adjoining suites. Both rooms were equally stunning and tucked away in a corner wing two floors from the top. Setha figured it was probably possible not to be found if quartered in such quiet, exquisite luxury.

"Guess they had quite a job cut out for them," Khouri said once he'd tipped the porter and walked him to the door. He took a seat on the back of one of the eggshell-colored sofas and watched her at the double doors leading out to the balcony that spanned their rooms.

"I resent that remark, Mr. Ross. Don't group all us 'sisters' in the same category based on your experiences," Setha drawled, her attention still focused past the balcony doors.

He bowed his head and smiled. "You have to admit it, though."

"Admit what?" She laughed.

"That it's easy to get full of yourself when all your brothers' friends probably wanted a piece of you." The corners of his vivid gaze crinkled on a wince as the words touched his ears. "That came out wrong," he whispered with a playful grimace.

"Don't worry about it." She turned from the balcony doors. "That's pretty much the same way Sam put it. He told me that there were men who based love on looks because that's what they truly valued." Her dark eyes adopted a faraway gleam. "He said a man like that doesn't know love at all and wouldn't want me for long if that's all he was basing his feelings on."

"Sam sounds like a smart guy."

Setha shrugged. "He's got his moments."

Laughter rumbled.

"He's right, you know?"

The view wore thin for Setha then and she sauntered close, not stopping until she stood between his thighs where he sat on the sofa. "I wondered if you could be put in that category." She scrunched up her nose and scrutinized him.

"I wondered that myself."

His admission made her heart flip woefully but she appreciated his honesty. "And?" she forced herself to ask.

A furrow found its way between Khouri's sleek long brows as he studied every curve and feature of her face. "No man could see you and not be stopped by the way you look. I've chosen women—lots of women—because of their looks." He shook his head, his bright eyes never leaving her face. "This time...it just doesn't feel like I've done that."

She nodded. "Maybe it's because you...saved me." She smirked over the phrasing.

Khouri considered her point, and then shook his head again. "Sorry—it doesn't feel like that, either."

She snuggled into him then, circling his neck with her arms and raking her nails across his nape where baby-fine hair tapered. "What does it feel like?" she asked.

Corded bands of muscle flexed in his forearms when they locked about her waist. "Feels like heaven."

No further time was wasted on discussion. Khouri knotted a portion of her hair in his fist and pulled her into his kiss. Playing a game of hide-and-seek, he thrust his tongue deep, but refused her attempts to entwine hers about his. Still seated on the back of the sofa, he took advantage of his comfortable position. Cupping her butt beneath the denim capris that neatly encased it, he cradled the firm globes in wide palms and drew her farther into the embrace of his thighs.

Setha didn't argue when he broke the kiss once she realized he'd done it in order to glide his mouth down the slope of her neck. She angled her head to give him more room to explore while simultaneously nuzzling her ample breasts into his chest.

Khouri uttered something low, guttural that seemed to surge up from the depths of him. Moments later, he was scooping her up still cradling her bottom in his hands.

She felt a cushioned, luxurious surface beneath her back—not the sofa as she'd anticipated, but one of the beds in the plush, airy suites. Khouri had placed her in the center of a queen-size four-poster and directed every ounce of his attention on solving the mystery of how to relieve her of her clothing. He had her half out of them when the phone on the nightstand began to ring. It rang loudly.

"Son of a..." His voice held the definite tinge of a growl then. Reluctantly, he drew his face from the valley between Setha's breasts—bared once he'd pressed open the front clasp of her bra—reached over and snatched the receiver from its mount.

Setha was moving to give him room to handle the call and found herself held between his body and the thigh he dropped across hers. Patiently, she waited, listening to him thanking someone after he'd answered the call in an obviously gruff tone.

"Business?" she asked, once he was done with the call.

"Of sorts."

His vague response had Setha puffing out her cheeks in slight agitation.

"Do you mind me asking what this part of the trip is supposed to accomplish?"

"Hopefully, we'll come away with a few more locales for the campaign." He returned to her breasts, outlining them with the tip of his nose.

Setha sighed, deliciously affected by the delicate bath his tongue was giving to her nipples.

"And since you're the woman I love…" He fell into thoroughly suckling her firmed nipples then.

"Khouri…" She ground her hips against his while pushing more of herself into his mouth.

He looked down at her then. "Since you're the woman I love, hopefully we'll come away knowing more about each other."

Onyx gaze dreamy, she raked her fingers through the curls smattering his head. "I hope you realize that downtown Houston isn't the most private place to do that."

His smile was devilment personified. "You'd be surprised at what a man can do when he's driven."

"Such as?" Her voice was a taunting purr.

He plied her with another long kiss. He placed the same attention upon her nipples and then drew back.

"Rest up for tonight," he ordered, dropping a kiss to her temple and leaving her alone in the bed.

Avra was out enjoying the downtown Houston scene as well but it had nothing to do with the Melendez account. She was having drinks with a well-known developer who wanted to work on a new campaign to highlight his projects in *Ross Review*.

"I should've thought of this a long time ago," Rauli Atkins said when he returned from the bar with their drinks.

"Surely, you've advertised in this area before?" Avra sipped her vodka straight and nodded her satisfaction at the taste.

Rauli shrugged. "*Some* advertising. Nothing like what I'd want to do with *Ross*."

"I'm glad you think we're what you're looking for."

"You've got a lot to do with that." His brown stare traveled appreciatively across her alluring features and the silver-toned off-shoulder blouse that accentuated her dark skin. "You make business seem like anything but."

Avra lifted her glass in toast. "Well then, to me!"

Rauli followed suit. "I'll drink to that!"

The couple took deep sips and set down their glasses with laughter carrying between them. Avra was glad she'd accepted the offer to meet Rauli in the city. The good feelings lasted right up until she caught sight of Samson Melendez…and his date.

Sam was on a mission to get Avra Ross out of his head and prove his sister wrong. Sure, she fascinated him, he thought while grimly following his date and a waitress to one of the tables in the private club. A cool $500 held the seats reserved for the evening. The wasted money had done nothing to improve his mood.

So he was fascinated by Avra Ross, so what? She wasn't the first or last woman he'd be fascinated by.… With no small effort, he ignored the niggling little voice in the back of his skull that told him how very wrong he was about that.

"Dos Equis." He barely grunted the drink request to the bubbly waitress.

He was only fascinated because he wanted her in bed. Once he had her there, he'd be done with her. There was nothing more to it than that. That is, until he saw her across the crowded club they'd both picked that night to visit.

Without a word to his date, Sam crossed the floor toward Avra and her companion. He didn't need to announce himself, she had already noticed him—tried to laugh over something her date had said, but failed.

"Well, well," she spoke through clenched teeth, and then smiled at the man seated to her left. "Sam Melendez, this is—"

"What's goin' on, Rau?" Sam was already extending a hand.

"Sam!" Rauli got to his feet and returned the hearty shake. "I was hopin' we'd see each other before I left town."

"When are you headed out?"

"Couple of days."

"Stop by the office before you go."

"Count on it. Hey? Join us?"

"Rauli—" Avra interrupted.

"I insist," Rauli stifled Avra's words of discouragement. He squeezed her shoulder. "One drink? I'm gonna run to the bar--waitress is as slow as Hades."

"Proud of yourself?" Avra leaned against the silver-barred back of her chair and kept a steely gaze trained on the crowded room, "I'm not your baby sister. I don't need your protection from all the big bad boys out there." She maintained her cool when he bent low, crowding her at the table.

Sam placed one hand on the table, the other on the back of Avra's chair. "I know you don't need that. Can I help it if I saw someone I know?"

Avra reached for her clutch purse. "Then I'll just leave y'all to catch up." He made no effort to move his hands. The look in his ebony stare told her not to even try moving then.

"Jealous, Sam?"

"We were workin' together."

"And there was no need to check on me."

"I see—" his smirk held more tension than humor "—because there's more to this than business."

"*That's* none of your business." She stared fixedly at the silver wristwatch glinting beneath the cuff of his shirt. "Do you mind?"

Sam straightened. Avra took advantage of newfound freedom to bolt from the table.

Sam kept his vicious curse muffled. Rolling his eyes, he managed to smile in the face of his stupidity. "Nice, Sam. Nice."

Setha gave in to the air of decadence swirling through her when Khouri knocked on the adjoining suite door when he came to collect her for dinner that evening. Although business was their primary reason for being there, she'd hoped the dress she wore might encourage him to forgo their responsibilities and enjoy their rooms a bit more.

"We're already dressed," he reasoned.

Setha waved a hand toward the chic silk amber dress. The draping neckline teased an admirer with a glimpse of rising bosom. "This is very easy to get out of," she boasted.

"I'll bet." Khouri's tone held a resigned quality. His vivid stare settled more than once to the frock's flirty neckline.

"Your expression tells me you might be willing to take my suggestion." She leaned against the door connecting their rooms and flattered him with a provocative stare.

Khouri relaxed against the doorjamb, easing his hand into a trouser pocket. "Is that what it's telling you?"

She nodded eagerly. "Uh-huh." She curled her fingers about the tail of the coffee-colored shirt hanging outside his trousers.

It was easy to entice him into the kiss. She skimmed her tongue across the even ridge of his teeth, hungry for the taste and smell of him. She moaned quietly, darting her tongue out to play with his, and then pressing her lips heatedly against his.

Khouri's hands grazed her satiny thighs en route to her derriere beneath the dress. He squeezed her into him and they merged into a scandalously wanton kiss right there on the threshold of their rooms.

"Yes, please," she breathed when he clutched her tight as though he were about to lift her and take her to his bed or hers. Her heart thudded its anticipation and she kissed with a hungrier fire. Threading her fingers into the curls at the base of his neck, she drove her tongue insistently against his.

"Khouri, please…"

"Honey, wait." He gave in to a few more seconds of

the kisses and fondling. Then he grunted and planted a hard, long kiss to her forehead. "Business first, okay?"

Setha could hear the torture in his voice, but she knew his mind was set. Obligingly, she nodded.

He brushed his thumb across her mouth and the lip-stick smudged there. "Fix this," he whispered with a heart-stopping smile.

"Have I been here before?" Setha wondered, twirl-ing a lock of her blue-black hair about her thumb while leaning against Khouri as they took the elevator to the hotel's skyline restaurant.

Khouri observed the passing night view of down-town Houston from the glass-encased elevator. "Doubt it. They serve dinner here, you know?"

His dig at her "adversity" to eating out was taken in good humor. Still, Setha couldn't resist shoving her elbow into his ribs.

"So you're thinking of a dinner shot?" She worked her hand through the crook of his elbow.

He barely shrugged. "Sort of."

They were greeted by the host who took them into the restaurant by way of the kitchen. They lingered there for a while. Khouri spent close to ten minutes shaking hands and speaking with the cooks and a few of the waiters.

The host led them to yet another elevator that car-ried them to the roof.

"Aah..." Setha understood.

"I like this one more for an evening shot," he told her, inhaling the crisp air that met them as they left the elevator.

"I can see why..." Setha inhaled as well, tossing

back her hair for an unobstructed view. There was no denying the beauty of downtown Houston while it was lit by the abundance of light.

"Sherman will be with you soon." The host left them with the name of their server.

"How is it you're so well-known here and *we've* never met?" Setha asked once they were alone on the roof.

Khouri walked over to meet her at the railing. "Everything in its own time, I guess."

"And now you've closed down a restaurant for me," she said after they had enjoyed the view in silence for a while.

Khouri chuckled, stroking the back of his hand across his jaw. "I'm not exactly a closing-down-restaurants type of guy."

"Mmm…" Setha closed her eyes to savor a strong breeze in her face. "You're just a closing-down-rooftop-dining-rooms-and-giving-me-my-own-exclusive-sky-view kind of guy?"

"Exactly." His arm banded about her waist and he pulled her into a kiss that ended when the waiter cleared his throat.

"Sherm!" Khouri greeted the waiter who'd been in the main dining room when they'd walked through the kitchen earlier. "Do you mind if I order?" he asked Setha once he and Sherman shook hands.

Setha was already waving her consent and then turned back to enjoy the extraordinary view. When he returned to tug her back into his embrace, she melted into Khouri's secure unyielding frame.

"So about why we've never met… It *is* weird, given how close our dads are. And we've never had so much as a playdate." He nuzzled his handsome face into the crook of her neck.

Setha laughed hearty and long. "I'm tryin' to imagine Sam and Avra together in a sandbox."

Laughter roared on the rooftop for a while.

"You know I actually heard Sam asking my dad about that when he and Avra started working on the campaign."

"And?"

She snuggled deeper into Khouri's chest. "He said there was a time in his life when he wanted his family life separated from his business life. I guess our dads started off as associates—they were friendly ones but maybe the relationship didn't really take off 'til later. Maybe they decided to just keep their entire relationship private—removed even from family." She shrugged, nuzzling her head beneath his chin. "At least they had each other when they lost our mothers."

"Yeah…." Khouri kissed the top of her head and they shared the view in silence.

After a late start the next morning, Khouri and Setha took in the offerings of their city. They even worked in a tour of Houston's Downtown Aquarium. The marvel was home to over two hundred species of marine life.

Following a robust walk over the six-acre spread, the couple stopped for lunch at the aquarium's restaurant where they spent over an hour next to the 150,000-gallon aquarium that cast liquid shimmers of illumination from the mellow, colorful depths of the water. Only after leaving, did they realize that they had been so captivated by the beauty of the aquatic life behind the glass tank they had totally neglected lunch.

* * *

"Do you think this is wise? A great view is what got us in trouble at lunch," Setha remarked when she joined Khouri on the balcony.

They'd decided on dinner from the patio of their adjoining suites. The private pool and breathtaking fire pit were definite attention getters though.

Khouri was clicking off the room's cordless phone when Setha arrived outside. Once again, he'd handled ordering the evening's menu. Barefoot, he spanned the patio and came to rest against the balcony railing.

"I'm pretty sure our stomachs are too empty to be ignored for much longer. The view will keep." He quieted then, massaging his jaw and settling deep into his thoughts.

"What?" She tilted her head while making the inquiry. The flaring hem of her dress stretched against the consistent breeze while she moved deeper onto the balcony.

Khouri shook his head, still stroking his jaw. "Thinkin' about before—what we were talking about— how we never got to know each other as kids."

"Right." She spoke in an encouraging tone, patiently waiting for him to share more. She took a seat on the chaise closest to the fire.

She and Khouri had both taken to lounge clothes for the evening. Her tie-dyed lounger perfectly complemented his navy blue sleep pants which were his only attire. The scene was set for conversation and more delightful things.... Setha absorbed the warmth from the fire. She massaged her fingertips into her bare arms and considered his point.

"Things were so great when we were kids," she remembered in a dreamy tone that didn't quite bring complete ease to her expression. "All that was before Ma... We were always going places, doing things. We stayed busy and excited. Living lives *worthy* of the children of Danilo Melendez. Hmph." She looked toward the fire as if it held some mystical secret that she craved the answer to.

Setha continued, "I was there when he and Sam had that talk. Daddy said he didn't want to be reminded of what it took to get where we were—to achieve the lives and lifestyles we had been blessed with. I think him seeing your dad and vice versa was too much of a reminder."

"But a reminder of what?" Khouri frowned. "They didn't grow up together."

Setha braced her hands back against the chaise. "I don't think Sam got an answer to that one, either."

The bell rang—room service. Khouri went to answer it while Setha eased down on the chaise and continued her observation of the fire. Shortly afterward, Khouri returned with a loaded cart of food. Rib eyes, baked potatoes that were pepper sprinkled and brimming with thick sour cream and melting butter. A basket of hard rolls, sautéed vegetables and salad rounded out the meal.

Setha scooted to the edge of the chaise and checked the wine. There was a hearty merlot, a great accompaniment for the steak. Massive blueberry muffins waited for dessert.

She smiled up at Khouri. "Where's yours?"

Later, with full stomachs, and a not-so-full bottle of wine, the lovers shared the rest of the drink and studied the fire that showed no signs of dwindling. Setha leaned back into Khouri's arms as he lay close, spooning her into his hard body.

"After Ma passed…Daddy he…he just shut down. He didn't want to kill himself, but it was clear he didn't have much interest in living." She shivered, in spite of the fire.

"I remembered him talking about your dad." She kissed his hand. "He was the biggest help after we all nagged him about getting out again. Mr. Basil had lost his wife, too—so there was that connection. A new one."

"And still they never brought us all together as kids." Khouri murmured the words into her hair.

"Well…" She closed her eyes against the heat. "Ma had so many friends—a lot of them we had never met. Not until the funeral…"

"Doesn't matter." His arms flexed about her curves like twin bands of iron. "We know each other now."

Setha turned to her back. "I've enjoyed getting to know you."

He trailed his thumb across her mouth, down her chin to the hollow at her collarbone. "There's a lot more to know."

"Really?" Biting her lip in a purely girlish manner, she stifled a giggle. "Such as?"

Khouri responded, nibbling the lip she bit down on. She opened her mouth, craving his kiss. She was so thoroughly absorbed in that act that she was delightfully stunned by his fingers when he thrust them high inside her.

The flaring hem of the lounger bunched about her waist. Setha wiggled her hips, desperate to be free of the stretchy fabric and the panties beneath it. Her wish was half filled when Khouri pushed the dress down to her breasts, baring the rest of her once he removed her panties.

Setha rotated herself on the chaise until Khouri imprisoned her thighs in his powerful grip. He kept them apart to savor her taste, thrusting his tongue inside her repeatedly as her moisture built. She tried to relieve herself of her dress, but Khouri held the garment in his fist at her breasts.

When he'd brought her to the brink of orgasm, his fist flexed around the fabric and he drew her up to sit. He released his hold, silently encouraging her to finish undressing herself.

The garment was barely over her head before his mouth was on her breasts, hungrily devouring the sweetness of the dark molasses-drenched mounds.

"Khouri…" She straddled his lap. "Foreplay later— you now." She ground herself against his erection.

Ravenous for her, he needed no further urgings. He hooked a hand behind her knee, and drew her back down to the chaise. Before doffing his sleep pants, he pulled a condom from the pocket. The pants fell in a heap near the pool.

Setha shivered, not from the sudden nip in the air, but from the sudden fullness between her legs. Protection gloved his erection seconds before he sheathed it inside her.

Khouri welcomed the weakness overtaking him. All strength flowed to his sex and he took her with a rigor that made him feel faint yet powerful at once.

On the verge of another orgasm, Setha was determined to have it. She gripped his ass to keep him where he was. Selfishly, she took what she wanted. Khouri didn't mind, of course. He was more than happy to be all that she needed.

Chapter 16

Setha watched Khouri's car until it rounded the bend leading off her property. After breakfast in bed at the Seasons, he'd just dropped her off at her home in River Oaks. Once his car was out of sight, she floated into the house. Yes, she was definitely floating.

Inside the house, she rested against the front door when she pushed it shut behind her. She tried to snap herself out of the haze she felt wrapped in, but it was no use. She was completely and deliciously enveloped in something warm and desire filled, courtesy of Khouri Ross.

She pushed off the door, hugging herself as she strolled into her home. Standing in the center of her living room, she kept hugging herself then, not out of contentment but out of mild agitation. The fact that she was alone at home hit her for the first time and she wasn't contented by the fact.

She loved Khouri. She missed him. How had that happened and how had it happened so fast? Her love life hadn't been a sob story before she had met him. Sure, none of the men she had expressed an interest in had lasted very long but she hadn't been all that upset over the fact. She had her family and her work. It had been enough.

Now, Khouri was there and there she hoped he'd remain.

When Setha walked into the *Ross Review* a few mornings later, she was on the arm of another man she loved.

"Play nice," she whispered to Samson and laughed softly when he growled in reply.

Khouri and Setha had arranged a meeting with ad execs from Ross and Melendez to present final proposals on the new Machine Melendez campaign.

Setha's fingers clenched slightly around Sam's bicep when they both stepped into the conference room. She saw Khouri on the other side. They'd both been busy over the past few days—scarcely having time to speak to one another even by phone. The scouting trip and all the meetings to set up the campaign had cut seriously into work time on their other responsibilities. This day would be the first they'd seen each other since returning from the trip.

Sam had stopped off to speak with a few people from his team. That left Setha time to choose her spot at the long table. She felt a hand at her waist less than a minute later.

"Mr. Ross, good morning," she said, having turned to face him.

Agitated by the stiff greeting, Khouri barely stifled his grimace. "When the hell are you going to tell them about us?"

"Soon." She pressed her lips together and moved closer when he rolled his eyes. "Khouri, I promise. I just want to wait a little longer until everything's blown over."

"Uh-uh." He propped an index finger below her chin. "You make it faster than that."

She shifted her weight to the other pump-shod foot. "Is there a rush?"

"Damn straight there is." A softer element merged onto his striking features. "I'd like very much to kiss you."

She smiled.

He studied the small pearl bracelet at her wrist. "Everything's all right at the house?" he asked.

Setha frowned, thinking the question strange until she realized he was asking about the new security system.

"I guess it's fine." She sighed, clearly not very impressed by the high-tech gadgetry he'd requested for her home.

"You're remembering to set the alarm when you leave?" Absently, his thumb stroked the bend of her elbow that was revealed thanks to the capped sleeves of her aqua-blue dress. "It can take some getting used to," he cautioned.

Setha blinked. "I have to do that?"

"Seth…" Khouri massaged his forehead.

"Hold on," she piped up, turning to search her bag for the phone. "Let's see… RJ told me how…." She found the mobile and hit a few buttons. She laughed then and turned to show Khouri the faceplate. ALARM SET it read.

He didn't seem impressed. "Damn thing ain't worth havin' if you won't even use it."

She eased closer. "Like you said, it could take some getting used to." She tugged his lapel when he remained stiff. "Stop worrying, will you? I'm quite capable of takin' care of myself when my gorgeous knight with the fantastic cologne isn't on the premises. Come on…." She tugged his lapel again and kept tugging until he smiled.

"Damn nosy…" Avra said when she slammed her portfolio to the table next to where Samson had claimed his spot and sat staring across the room at Setha and Khouri.

"Avra…" he groaned, eyes raking her body appreciatively even as his mouth curved into a grimace. "Just when I thought my day couldn't start off any worse."

"Tell me about it." Avra wore an equally disdainful grimace. She pulled out the chair next to Sam.

"My sister's sitting there."

"What is this? The first grade?" She plopped down in the chair.

Samson smiled, bringing to life the faint appealing crinkles next to his pitch-black gaze. "Didn't think you were brave enough to sit next to me." He took his time surveying the rise of her bosom at the keyhole cut of the coral frock she wore. "You know you've got everybody here thinkin' I'm the big bad wolf or somethin'."

"I haven't said a thing." Avra lent an intentional airiness to her voice. "My group's smart enough to recognize a nasty bully when they see one."

"Oh, I bet they are." Sam focused on a small tuft of lint clinging to his tie. "Workin' for you I'm sure they're experts at spotting bullies. Especially nasty ones."

"You—"

"Hush now, meeting's starting." He turned his chair toward the front of the room.

Avra debated on whether or not to slap the back of his head.

Khouri and Setha stood at the head of the table and thanked everyone for coming. They quickly brought the group up to speed on what they'd been doing.

"We've made a few minor changes in the overall 'focus' of the original campaign," Khouri said.

Setha was nodding her agreement. "We think we've come up with ideas everyone can be happy with."

Khouri raised a hand toward the far corner of the room. "We should thank Cleve Haskins and Eden Forrester from the Ross and Melendez art departments for getting this together so fast."

Khouri turned the floor over to the art directors who had basically used the previous shots and redrawn them to depict the new ideas. It was clear that all the meeting attendees were riveted on the proposal. Samson and Avra, so averse to making an agreement, seemed impressed by the presentation. Both sat straighter in their seats to view each new slide more intently. At the conclusion, Khouri and Setha graciously accepted applause and compliments.

"So when do we begin shooting the spots?" Sam asked.

"We'll be ready to start as soon as the next few weeks." Setha perched her hip to the conference table.

"That is, if you're free to visit the locations and give approval beforehand."

"That good for you, Av?" Khouri called out to his sister.

On the spot, the two execs couldn't refuse and gave their murmurs of approval. There was more applause and the meeting adjourned shortly after.

Avra left the meeting as soon as it ended. She closed up in her office and began to pore over Wade Cornelius's notes as she'd done since visiting Vita Arroyo over a week earlier. One booming thud hit her door a split second before it opened. Avra barely had time to swing her legs off the sofa.

"It was closed for a reason," she said when Sam filled her doorway, and then went back to reviewing her notes.

Sam waited a beat after pushing the door closed before he spoke. "I didn't send my sister over here to spend time on her back."

Avra kept her eyes on the page she studied, but her mouth tilted into a smile. "Sam, Sam. You know this jealous bit really doesn't become you. Are you upset that we didn't treat you to the same service?"

"How long's it been goin' on?"

"Hell, Sam, how should I know?" She crossed her legs at the ankles on the sofa cushions. "I haven't had time to follow 'em around with a flashlight and document the rendezvous, you know?" She winced and set aside the notes. "Do you have somethin' against my brother?"

"I don't." He pointed a finger in her direction. "Everybody knows he's a good guy—best prospect Seth's had on her arm in…hell, ever." He shrugged. "We just like to know what's goin' on."

"Why? So y'all can ruin it with your bullying?" Avra waved at him like she was fanning a fly. "Sisters don't like to have the buzzards circlin' 24/7, Sam."

The smile he wore only added a more dangerous element to his bronzed face. He settled his heavy frame to the arm of the sofa.

"You get no argument from me." His eyes raked the length of her bare legs. "But if you were in my shoes, you may agree that some of you do need to be kept under lock and key."

"Jesus, no wonder you're single."

Sam reached down to squeeze her foot. "See you in Kemah."

When he left, Avra didn't try to ignore the tingles in her foot from where his hand had squeezed. Hissing a curse, she reached for the notes but used them to fan herself as she released an unsteady breath.

Khouri didn't need to be directed to the table where his lunch partners waited. Lovely and high-spirited, the women talked and laughed boisterously with seemingly no regard for all the attention—male attention—they drew. It'd be difficult for any man to have trouble signaling them out from a crowd.

"Show you to the table, K?"

"Nah, thanks, Ned." Khouri shook hands with the restaurant host.

Fiona saw her brother and nudged her sister who was still talking. In unison, they waved and smiled even more brightly for the man approaching their table.

When Khouri got there, he was tackled by hugs, kisses and whispers of congratulations. "What's wrong with y'all?" He used a napkin to wipe two shades of lipstick from his cheek.

"Well, Av told us you were seeing Setha Melendez," Raquel said once they'd taken their seats.

"Nice goin', Khouri. She's very pretty." Fiona's eyes sparkled as she raved.

"So what's with all the congratulations?"

The women exchanged frowns.

"Well, you *are* gonna ask her to marry you, right?"

"What?" Khouri leaned closer to Fiona as though he'd misheard her.

"You took her up on the roof," Raquel noted.

"What's that got to do with—"

"Marta and Avra told us you took her to the roof."

"I—"

"And you never take any women up there."

"I—"

"Well, he takes *us* up there," Fiona reminded her sister.

"You two—"

"Well, no women except family," Raquel countered.

Khouri let his fist hit the table, causing everything to jump, including his sisters. "That doesn't mean marriage, dammit." He rubbed his forehead.

Rocky and Fiona scooted their chairs closer to their brother. Both studied him in awe.

"You're really in love with her," Rocky breathed.

Khouri continued to massage his head. "Is this why y'all wanted to have lunch?"

"Well, *yeah!*" Fiona tugged at the cuff of his suit coat.

"Sweetie, this is so great!" Raquel moved to hug Khouri.

"We haven't even known each other that long." Khouri didn't know why he was bothering to explain, but thought it might help to try.

Fiona waved off the explanation, of course. "It doesn't take long to fall in love."

Khouri moaned. "Lord…"

"You guys are seeing each other though, right?" Raquel still required confirmation.

"We are but—" He closed his eyes, until the women's tickled laughter had subsided—somewhat. "Please, y'all, don't go blabbin' this to everybody and their mother. She hasn't even told her family yet."

"We won't tell a soul," Raquel swore.

"We promise," Fiona added and raised her right hand for good measure.

"Good grief." Again, Khouri massaged his forehead.

"Get you a drink, sir?" the waiter asked when he approached.

"Heineken," Khouri grumbled. "And keep 'em comin'."

"So when do we get to meet her?" Fiona asked.

"I think I met her once…maybe—some charity thing. That's what she does, right?" Raquel asked her brother.

Khouri only nodded.

"Wasn't anything formal. I didn't have a chance to talk to her or anything." Raquel was talking to Fiona then.

"Well, Khouri?" Fiona challenged. "We can't wait to welcome her to the Ross clan." She beamed.

He shook his head. "Don't y'all think the family has enough women?"

Fiona slapped her brother's arm. "No such thing."

* * *

"You've never taken any of my sage advice during all our years as friends." Basil studied the shot glass of tequila he'd taken from Danilo. "Why do you want it now?" he asked.

Danilo finished his shot in a second and then let loose a slight cough. "Whether I've wanted it or not, it's always been *sage* advice." He massaged his chest where the liquor burned beneath his gray chambray shirt. "Sage advice is what I need right now."

"You think someone at Melendez is responsible for the murders?"

"I don't. I've got to believe in my staff, Bas. I can't start suspecting them when so many of them are dying right in from me." Dan shook his head once, decisively. "I do think that whoever *is* responsible has a gripe with the company."

"You know that's a long, ugly list."

"Just tell me how I can get out in front of this, Basil."

The man shook his head. "The only thing *getting out in front of it* publicly will do is make you look like you're trying to hide something." He downed the shot.

"Well, hell, Bas, what options does that leave me with then?"

"Leaves you with the truth."

Dan straightened. "What are you saying?"

"I'm saying, you need to do everything you can to help the police find out who's behind this mess. Forget about the press and your image this time—they can wait until after this thing is solved."

"What are you saying, Basil?" Dan repeated, more firmly that time.

Basil studied the empty glass. "I think you know.

Wade's death, the murders…they're all connected. You remember what Wade uncovered when he researched that Holloway story."

"To hell with that." Dan began to pace the sitting room. "It was decades ago when John… When all that happened."

"It was *started* decades ago." Basil's expression hardened, he smoothed an unsteady hand across his close-cut hair. "We both know it didn't end decades ago, don't we?"

"I don't see how that'll help solve or stop these murders."

"I do. This isn't all coincidence, Dan. The answers are right there."

"And you really want to go rooting around in all that again?" Dan probed. "You of all people who wanted to sever as many ties to that past as possible?"

"Well, I didn't do too good of a job with that, did I?" Basil showed a rueful grin. "The *Review* has pretty much been MM's own personal PR company, hasn't it?"

"And I thank you for that, old friend."

Basil set his shot glass to the coffee table. "When you come 'round to my way of thinking, let me know. I'll support you one-hundred percent."

Silence captured the room then. Dan continued to pace while Basil reclined on a couch with his shoes propped on the coffee table.

"Still think my advice is sage?" Basil asked.

Dan broke into contagious laughter. "Still sage and still hard to take!"

Laughter rumbled slow but steady between the friends.

* * *

"Damn," Setha hissed a curse when the doorbell rang just as the endgame was being revealed in the spy thriller she was watching. Pausing the movie, she ran barefoot down the hall from the TV room to the front door. In a huff, she whipped open the door and came down off her anger when she saw that it was Khouri.

His expression was less than gleeful. "Did you even bother to see who it was first?"

Setha's expression answered the question in the negative. She moved aside when he stepped forward to enter.

"I was just watching a movie." She hiked a thumb across her shoulder. "Can I get you something to eat?"

"Not hungry."

"A drink?"

"No."

She bit her lip and twisted one foot to the side. "Are you sleepy?"

Shrugging slowly, Setha closed the tiny distance between them and linked her arms about his neck. "Wanna go to bed anyway?" She stood on her toes and coaxed his mouth open with the tip of her tongue. She kissed him greedily and gasped when he clutched her butt beneath the black boy shorts she wore.

"Stop..." she whined, when he tried to ease her back.

"Later, okay?"

"No...."

"Tell me what you were watching."

"Well, I hate to ruin it for you if you haven't seen it. *The Sum of All Fears?*" She moved back to watch him.

"Oh, yeah, it's one of my favorites." He nodded, trailing his thumb along her jaw. Absently, he named a few other movies in the genre. He asked if she'd seen them when he was clearly more interested in watching her face.

"I wouldn't have pegged you for a movie buff."

Khouri shrugged, toying with her hair then. "Now that's one more thing you know about me."

"I have the feeling there's a lot more to learn." She clasped her hands behind her back. "Wonder how long that'd take?"

"You may not want to know all that," he warned, leaning against the front door.

"I'd want to know. I'd want to know it all." She stood on her toes and grazed her lips across his jaw.

"Could take a while." He moved to cup her derriere again.

"Mmm… I don't care…."

"Could take a lifetime…." He nuzzled her ear until she stepped back to watch him. "Marry me." His words held a dreamy, coaxing undercurrent.

"Khouri…" She told herself to blink, but couldn't manage it.

His gaze didn't waver. "I'll wait, Setha—as long as it takes for your answer."

"Yes," she breathed, moving close to grasp the open collar of the short-sleeved denim shirt he wore. "Yes, yes…."

Nuzzling her face again, he buried his hands in her hair. "This is real fast, you know?"

"Yes, yes…." she repeated, smoothing her hands up his chest around his neck and into his hair.

"I love you."

"I love you, too."

"You're gonna have to tell your family," Khouri said while they hugged.

Setha released a playful groan. "Oh, no…."

Chapter 17

"What are y'all doin'? Come on in," Setha told her brothers when she returned from the kitchen to find the two men still in the foyer.

Paolo and Lugo wore twin scowls when they glanced their sister's way before turning back toward the lighted box near the door.

"What the hell's this?" Lugo asked, referring to the security panel.

"We'll discuss it when Daddy and Sam get here!" She whirled away from the foyer.

"Why? What is it?" Paolo persisted and slanted his younger brother a glare.

The men already knew what the box was. The real question was *why* was it there? Setha was in no mood to get into it then or later for that matter.

Unfortunately, the time for stalling had passed. She was getting married. The idea almost made her double over from excitement. Everything had happened so fast, but she had never been happier. Her family was sure to be thrown for a loop or three. Setha believed it was good to shake them up a bit every now and then.

"What the hell's goin' on, Set?" Paolo demanded.

"What the hell are you grinnin' for?" Lou asked.

Setha was saved from answering when the bell rang again. Danilo and Samson had arrived together. Setha pulled open the door, wearing an even brighter grin.

"Look at this!" Dan cried, happy to see his youngest child looking so elated. He laughed when Setha threw herself into his arms.

"Why won't my key work?" Sam wasn't so gleeful.

"I had the locks changed." Setha moved out of her father's embrace. She took his arm and tugged him toward the living room.

"Everything all right, *niña?*"

"Hey, what's this thing on the door?" Sam called, having spared a moment to observe the "box" before he followed his father and sister toward the living room.

"We gotta *discuss* it!" Lugo called from the bar.

In less than a minute, Setha was surrounded by the men in her family. Only Danilo's voice remained calm.

"Tell us what's going on, *bonita.*"

Setha wiped damped palms on the apron covering her flaring denim skirt. "It's a security system."

"What the hell for?" Paolo asked.

"I'm getting married."

Silence and blank stares met the announcement.

"Does that require security?" Lugo asked.

Paolo shrugged. "*You* know what she's like to live with. The guy might need it."

Dan took his daughter's hand. "Who is this man, *niña?*"

"Oh, Daddy, you'll like him." Setha pressed her hand to his cheek. "He's your best friend's son."

"Ross!" Sam bellowed.

Setha smiled, but kept eye contact with her father. "I know it's sudden but we—we love each other. I'm in love with him, Daddy, and—"

"Shh…" Dan stepped close, cupping Setha's chin and peering into her dark eyes with his own. He smiled after several quiet seconds. "Yes—" he nodded "—yes, you are, aren't you?"

Setha hugged him tight. "Thank you, Daddy."

"I didn't send you to *Ross* to bag a husband, Set," Samson blurted, watching the tender scene with a bland expression.

"*You* didn't send me to *Ross* at all. Daddy did." She plied Dan with a kiss to the jaw. "Thank you, Daddy." She leaned back against her father and fixed her brother with a smug look. "Don't get upset with me because I snagged Khouri and you can't close the deal with Avra."

The room roared with laughter.

"Soup's on!" Setha announced, clapping Sam's back as she waltzed from the room.

The family was well into the meal Setha had prepared. For several minutes after they sat down, all that could be heard was the scrape of silverware to plates, the crunch of chicken as someone bit into a succulent piece, or a lid clatter as it was moved from a dish to get another helping.

Setha smiled, eating from her place closest to where her father sat at the head of the rectangular table.

It was Lugo who broke the silence once he'd dipped out his third helping of spinach casserole. "So when do I get to meet this guy?"

"He wanted to be here." Setha poured more iced tea into her glass. "I asked him to let me handle this part."

"Let you *handle* it?" Sam barked from his seat at the opposite end of the table. He was still smarting over his little sister's dig about Avra. "Did you think we'd tear him apart or something?"

"You mean the way you've torn apart all the other ones?" She shook her head. "It wasn't like that—he really wanted to be here."

"Cool it, Sam," Paolo said while reaching for another chicken breast. "For once, she hasn't latched onto some dud. Khouri's a good guy, you know that."

"He made you get that system, didn't he?" Sam asked after he'd taken a few more forkfuls of rice pilaf. "Gotta be love. None of us been able to make you do it."

"Enough, Sam," Dan ordered.

"No, Daddy, Sam's right." Setha clinked her fork to her glass. "The system was Khouri's idea, but I should've already done it."

Suspicion slowly filled the eyes of the four men at the table. Setha could almost feel their stares boring into her and knew the time to finish the story was at hand.

"Someone's been following me."

The explosion Setha had expected after making the wedding announcement came through hotly then. Sam exploded, as did Paolo and Lugo. Setha could scarcely get a word in as they fired questions and admonishments her way. It was Danilo's firm, calm voice that finally cooled the younger men's raging tempers.

"What happened, *niña?*" He squeezed Setha's hand.

Hoping to thwart more exploding tempers, Setha made quick work of explaining what had been going on for the past several weeks. She told them how she'd met Khouri at the club and the circumstances of that meeting.

"You should've told us this, Set."

"Sam," Dan warned. "Do you know who it was, love?"

"His name's Carson Arroyo. I thought he was doing it for payback."

"Payback?" Lugo queried.

Setha dabbed her mouth with a linen napkin. "His dad worked for us. He was fired and then killed himself."

"I want you with me at least until after the wedding. I assume it won't be a long engagement?" Dan confirmed.

"Daddy, I—"

"No arguments, Setha."

She tilted her head, taking note of the rising temper in his gaze. In addition to the rage, she could also tell that fear lurked there.

Setha had never relished bringing worry to her family. Her father and brothers were always on edge when it came to her independence. It was one reason why she'd made it her mission to excel in so many male-dominated activities in an effort to convince them of her capabilities.

As angry as they were the night she told them about Carson Arroyo, Setha knew they were more frightened for her safety than anything. Her father was the only one who seemed to listen when she told him she didn't believe Carson was only after her.

Whatever had or would happen, she was happy to finally bring a touch of happiness.

The engagement party was held that weekend. Raquel had insisted on shutting down her club for the event. It was a smart idea as many of the bride's and groom's friends lived in the city. The decision saved them from long drives to Setha's place or turning Khouri's apartment upside down in preparation for the event.

The air was filled with laughter, music, conversation and the clink of bottles and glasses. The second level of Rocky Ross's was furnished with curved, cushiony sofas set around low coffee tables. Groups of no more than ten could gather for drinks and chatter while looking down at the lit stage and dance floor.

It was there that Setha got to know her future sisters-in-law a little better. The four young women cast off an impressive number of the opposite sex. Infectious laughter was at its height while the ladies dined on appetizers and enjoyed delicious drinks. Avra made a point of informing every man who even spoke to Setha that she was taken.

Fiona almost choked on the schnapps she sipped. "He was only telling her congrats, Av, jeez," she said when the embarrassed gentleman hurried away.

Avra threw up a lazy wave. "Can never be too careful," she slurred a bit.

Setha felt she'd laughed more that night than she had in a long time. She thought her family held the record for the most raucous characters. It seemed they were tied by her fiancé's people.

Avra was the loudest, brutally honest and most protective. Raquel was loud, brutally honest and possessed a wicked sense of humor. Fiona held a perfect balance of each of her elder sisters' traits with a generous topping of sarcasm. The added quality could cut a person down and have them rolling with laughter at once.

"Hope we won't be too much for you," Fiona cautioned.

Setha toyed with the silver-and-onyx beaded bangles that complemented the black asymmetrical frock she sported. She shook her head with confidence. "I think my crazy family's prepared me for anything."

"Hmph." Rocky tilted back her Sam Adams. "Don't be too sure. We can be hard to handle."

"Aah…so your brother wasn't exaggerating, huh?"

The sisters pretended to be offended. They debated wildly among themselves about what basis Khouri could possibly have for thinking such a thing. Setha could barely sit up straight she was laughing so hard.

"We know this happened awfully fast," she admitted once the laughter eased off a tad. "My family was just as surprised by it."

Avra fidgeted with her gold earrings that dangled against her neck. "Did they try to talk you out of it?" She bit her lip once the question was asked.

"They didn't." Setha smiled on the memory of it. "I love your brother very much." She brought fist to chin and regarded them seriously. "It—it's strong and it shocked the hell out of me. I thought I knew mostly all there was to expect from men. Khouri showed me how wrong I was."

Raquel reached out to squeeze her hand. "We believe you." She looked to her sisters who nodded. "We believe you 'cause we see the same thing on Khouri's face when he looks at you."

"That surprises you?" Avra noticed Setha's expression. "Honey, we've never seen him so intense, so…set on any woman—ever."

"When we were down there on the floor, Khouri was watching you every time I looked his way," Fiona added.

"Mmm-hmm," Raquel confirmed, twisting a cheek-length lock of coiled hair around her finger. "He watches you like you're the only thing he sees."

"Really?" Setha didn't know if the schnapps was to blame or if happiness had her so loopy with delight.

"Mmm-hmm." Again, Raquel confirmed before finishing off what remained of her drink. "My brother watches you the way *your* brother watches my sister."

All eyes turned to Avra, who sat watching her tablemates blandly.

"What?" she said.

Khouri shook hands with Danilo Melendez when the man approached him in the circle where he stood having a drink with his soon-to-be brothers-in-law.

"Apologies again, sir, for the way we broke the news," Khouri said, shifting his bright eyes toward his father who had arrived along with Dan.

"Guess it's hard to learn your daughter's serious about someone, let alone that she's about to marry him," he said.

Everyone in the group chuckled even as they nodded.

Dan clapped Khouri's shoulder. "I think it would've been hard to hear were it anyone but you. Your reputation precedes you, son. I'm confident my little girl is in good hands. That is—" a sly look crept into his black stare "—if I can trust anything *this man* says." He tilted his head toward Basil. "And I've been trusting his word since before any of you were born."

The rumble of laughter between the six men didn't stop the serious element from creeping back in among them.

"We were just thanking Khouri for keeping Setha safe during this mess." Samson let his words trail into silence having noticed the meaningful look placed between his father and Basil Ross.

"Sam's right. Thank you, son." Dan extended his hand for another shake.

"Khouri Ross! Congrats, man." Chief of Detectives Brad Crest approached with a big grin.

"'Preciate it, Brad." Khouri clutched the man's hand in a hearty shake. "You're not leavin', are you?"

"Not just yet." Brad jingled the keys he'd pulled from his khakis. "But duty will be callin' soon, I'm afraid."

"Got anything to do with the murders?" Lugo asked.

"Nah, 'bout time for my shift, is all. Can enjoy myself a little longer though," he said with a sly wink.

"Anything new with the case, Brad?" Basil asked.

Brad was grim. "Our leads all *lead* to dead ends. Aside from the vics sharing the same address at one time, we've got scratch." He rubbed his fingers across blondish-brown eyebrows and winced. "Sorry the news isn't better."

"You're doing your best."

"Damn right," Basil agreed with Dan's encouraging words to Brad.

Amid the exchange, Khouri's eyes narrowed sharply as he watched his father thoughtfully. Eventually, he noticed Samson appeared to be doing the same in relation to his own dad. Tossing back another swig of his drink, Khouri wondered if Sam was asking himself why the men were taking such dismal news so...calmly.

Chapter 18

The drinks had flowed abundantly before and during the party. Now that the event was winding down, the *flowing* hadn't let up. Setha smiled on her way out of the bathroom stall, thinking how hard laughter and drinking were on the bladder.

The bathroom had cleared while she was in the stall. Setha appreciated the time alone to collect herself as well as her thoughts.

She was getting married! Who would have thought that a favor to her brother could have had such an outcome? It was as she'd told her soon-to-be sisters-in-law, she thought she knew most everything there was to know about men. How pleasantly Khouri had surprised her. She couldn't wait to begin her married life with him.

Opening her eyes, she closed them again believing too much drink was causing her to see things just then.

The smile she wore faded slowly as she focused on the image behind her in the mirror. She couldn't wait to share her life with Khouri Ross and standing there behind her was the man who meant to prevent that.

She made no sudden moves, not that she could have without stumbling on her heels thanks to her imbibed state.

Setha grimaced then on the irony of it all. Why did Carson Arroyo always have to catch her in her best shoes?

"Why are you here?" she asked, facing him defiantly through the mirror.

Walking forward, Carson bowed his head while leaning against the bathroom counter. He was thin, but wiry and Setha knew better than most how fast he was. She didn't dare move. Yet.

"I think you know what I'm doing here, Miss Melendez."

She wouldn't cower and turned slowly to face him, her defiance building. If she was about to die, the son of a b before her would damn well tell her the truth about why.

"This is revenge for your parents, isn't it?"

"You know nothing about my parents!" He could have spat across the room with the force of the venom in his words.

"I know how your father's suicide—death," she rephrased when his small dark eyes narrowed sharply. "I know how hard things got for your family afterward." She held her chin up. "I know you blame my family for that."

"As I said, you know nothing."

She frowned in response to his calm demeanor. "If this is about money, my father would see to it that you and your family are cared for. You have my word on that."

The man's calm demeanor vanished. His palm fell upon the marble countertop with a loud thwack. Standing erect then, he advanced on Setha as she stumbled back in retreat.

"I don't want the Melendez money! Blood money! Have you ever once wondered about your spoiled childhood, little princess? Ever thought about the people your father made his millions off of?" He smirked when she stumbled again. "Dan Melendez is about to see what it's like to have a debt he can't repay."

Carson hooked his finger around the bracelet at Setha's wrist. He jerked her close, his eyes carrying a wildness mirrored by the harsh curl of his lips. Panicked and angry, Setha struck out blindly, but did meet an intended target when it connected with his groin. He fell to his knees, mewling pathetically.

Awkwardly, and much too slowly, Setha made her way across his form that was crumpled at her feet. She ran for the bathroom door, but stopped to brace her hand along the wall when things began to spin.

"Come on, Seth." She forced herself to focus. Turning her head toward the noise, she prayed she was heading in the right direction.

Khouri laughed as loudly as anyone at the bawdy jokes that had gone back and forth at the table full of men. The bawdier the jokes got, the louder the laughter roared. Khouri wiped a tear from his eye and noticed his fiancée in the distance. She was walking—*trying* to walk—down the corridor leading from the restrooms.

He smiled, watching her press a hand along the wall

to keep her balance. He made a mental note to tease her about it later that night. He was lifting a hand to wave, when he saw her jerked back by the man who had stumbled up behind her.

"Son of a b," he breathed, his bright eyes narrowed to slits as he slammed down a fist on the table.

Everyone silenced.

"Get Brad," he told no one in particular and bolted off.

"Do it," Samson told Lugo, having witnessed what sent Khouri running. Seconds later, he and Paolo were doing the same.

Setha chose to use her heels that night instead of kicking them off. She was able to land the tip of one into Carson's calf when he pulled her down. Her wild kicking paid off. He was forced to release her and she ran. Refusing to get caught out in the alleyway again, she headed down the flight of stairs which led to the basement that served as the storage and kitchen area of the club.

"Figures," she breathed, finding the expansive space empty. The dull thud of music was a grim reminder that she was but a hair's breadth from safety. She needed to make her way back up to it. She remained cautious, keeping a lookout for Carson maneuvering in and out of the shadows. She'd made her way back around to the staircase and was on the third step leading to the main floor. She was stopped before she could reach the fourth step.

Setha shrieked, prepared to fight again when he released her, pushing her down to the concrete flooring. Setha prepared to scramble, but reconsidered when she saw the gun aimed at her face.

"You don't have to do this, Carson." Her words carried in the vastness of the space.

"Why?" He sneered, flexing his fingers about the gun handle. "Because it's all in the past? Smart of you to realize that. It's in the past which means there's not a damn thing your daddy can do to give back my father's pride or my mother's dignity."

"But why?" she blurted in a whisper.

Carson could have passed his smile off as one of sympathy, were it not for the gun he cocked then. "Because you're your father's greatest treasure."

A shot went off, the ear-numbing ring of it vibrated through the space.

Setha waited for blinding pain and oblivion, but it never blossomed. Slowly, she opened her eyes to thin slits. They widened eventually at the sight of Carson Arroyo lying before her in a puddle of his own blood.

Setha felt herself jerked up—this time it was Khouri. His arm was banded across her. He kept her sealed tightly next to him, and rained kisses across her cheeks and the back of her neck. Dazedly, she watched Brad Crest kicking aside the gun Carson had carried.

"She all right?" he asked Khouri.

"Babe?" he murmured against her ear, squeezing her tighter when he felt her nodding.

Eventually, Setha's nods were delivered with more certainty. "Thank you," she said to Brad, noticing the gun he replaced in his holster. Shivers set in, turning her skin to gooseflesh. Seeking warmth and security, she pitched her face into Khouri's shirt clutching his arm desperately.

"I've got you," he murmured against her temple while he rocked her, "I've got you."

* * *

"And that's all he said?" Brad was asking while he took Setha's statement from Raquel's office at the club.

"I'm sorry." She shivered inside the blanket Khouri had wrapped her in. "I wish there was more I could tell—"

"Shh…now…" Brad waved a hand and eased a black leather-bound notebook into his back pocket. "You did enough."

"Amen to that." Khouri pressed his face into the top of her head.

Avra stood next to her sister's desk and scraped her thumbnail against her chin. Anyone who knew her would recognize the gesture as a clear sign of worry. She blinked away from Khouri and Setha to find Samson studying her. His obsidian stare was fixed and pensive. Grimacing, she crossed the room kneeling before Setha at the sofa.

"Me, Rock and Fee'll be over in the morning to check in on you, all right?"

Setha rubbed Avra's shoulder. "You don't have to do that."

"Well, that's what sisters do for each other," Avra retorted and then winked and moved up to kiss Setha's cheek. She squeezed Khouri's shoulder on her way past the sofa and out of the room.

"I'm goin' straight home," Avra said. She'd barely gotten down the hall when a hand closed on her arm. She knew it was Sam.

"Home sounds good," he said. "I'll be right behind you."

"That wasn't an invitation." She stopped walking and turned to glare.

His striking features softened under the mild humor. "I'd be very surprised if it were, darlin'."

He waved a hand to usher her on. Avra stifled her arguments, accepting the fact that she'd be keeping company with Samson Melendez that night.

Inside the office, Setha was still shivering in her fiancé's strong unyielding embrace. Khouri lifted her with an effortless display of strength. "Takin' you home," he grumbled.

"You found me." She stared up at him, her eyes searching his.

He kissed her mouth. "And I always will."

"Thank you."

"I love you."

She smiled. "You better."

Laughter hummed soft and sweet in the midst of the kiss they shared.

Chapter 19

One week later...

The upcoming nuptials between Khouri Adande Ross and Setha Bianna Melendez would be held at Samson Melendez's grand estate on the outskirts of Houston. Sam had insisted on every event of the wedding being held at his ranch. That included all the planning meetings and dinners.

Sam would hear no arguments or suggestions for other venues. He grudgingly allowed Setha to stay with her fiancé until the day before the wedding instead of having her move out of her home and in with him. Almost no one questioned the latter, knowing tensions still ran high following Carson Arroyo's death.

That afternoon was to be Setha's bridal shower. Sam, of course, insisted on the party being there at the ranch in spite of the previous arrangements that had been made. He had trucks sent to collect all delivered gifts from Setha's place and carry them out to his ranch.

Sam's overprotective nature, while sweet and beautiful to some, had worn thin with his father. Dan walked into Sam's study that afternoon to find him handling a phone call to Khouri. Danilo listened while his eldest son confirmed plans to have Setha brought to the ranch for the shower. Dan rapped his knuckles to the open door, the moment the call ended.

"Pop." Sam's greeting was polite but held an absent tone as he scribbled notes to a pad.

"What the hell are you doing?" Dan saw no need wasting time in getting to the point of his visit.

"Sir?" Sam set down his pen and gave his father a bewildered look.

Dan spread his hands and strolled slowly into the room. "All is well. There's peace—why go to all this trouble? You're acting crazier than the bride."

Sam leaned back in his desk chair and folded his arms across his chest. "Somethin's wrong with me makin' sure my sister's safe?"

"Your sister *is* safe." Dan's pitch-black stare narrowed. "And she has a very capable fiancé to see to her safety otherwise."

"I know that."

"So?" Dan moved to stand before the desk. "Why are you still on edge?"

Sam stood. From his height advantage , he watched his father knowingly. "Why don't you tell *me,* Papa?"

"Gentlemen?" Brad Crest knocked on the doorway and then waved. "'Scuse the interruption. Mr. Dan? Your people told me I could find you out here."

"What's up, B?" Sam asked, shifting his gaze back briefly toward his father.

Brad cleared his throat and jangled keys where they rested in his gray trousers pocket. "There's been another murder."

"Arroyo?" Sam asked, sounding as if he doubted the fact. "Someone he got to before he came after Setha?"

"Not likely, given the time of death."

"Which was?" Sam asked.

"Sometime between eight and ten last night. Seein' as how Arroyo's been dead for a week…"

"Son of a b…" Sam breathed, shoving at loose papers lying atop his desk.

"Is it another of my employees, Bradley?" Dan was asking as he stepped closer to the detective.

"I'm sorry, sir," Brad confirmed, his lips thinning as he nodded. "A Martino Viejo."

The heavy breath Dan expelled seemed to fill the room with sound.

"Pop?" Sam called, watching his father settle in the nearest chair.

"My God…" Dan bowed his head and shuddered.

"Should I pack this one, miss?"

Setha took the box the driver referred to. It didn't look like a gift if the plain brown packaging was any clue. The Kemah address on front brought a radiant smile to her face.

"Khouri!" Clutching the box to her chest, she raced down the hall to the TV room where he dozed.

"It's from Jim Beaumont," she told her fiancé once she'd shoved him awake.

"What?" Khouri spoke through a yawn, slowly locking in on the name.of the fragrance shop owner.

"Wake up," Setha urged, tugging insistently on the mushroom-colored polo shirt that hung outside his denim shorts.

Khouri sat up on the sofa. "What is it?"

Setha was already tearing into the box. "For the newlyweds," she announced, gathering the folds of the lavender-and-midnight-blue lounge dress and settling in Khouri's lap to read the rest of the card. "'For the newlyweds, a batch of…Texas *Tuffy* for the mister—'" She burst into laughter and fell back on the sofa.

Khouri rolled his eyes. "I'll kill him," he vowed, searching the box for his cologne.

"Wait, there's one for me…." Setha slapped his wrist. "'And for the missus, her own unique fragrance…Texas Love Song.'" She beamed and clutched the card to her chest.

"You can't kill a man *that* thoughtful." She sighed.

Khouri set aside the box and pulled his fiancée snug against his chest. "I've never been a fan of love songs." He nuzzled her ear.

Setha curled into him. "And now?" She angled her neck giving him more room to explore.

He cupped her neck in his palm. "They're growin' on me." He drew her into a throaty kiss. "Jim's still a dead man," he growled when his mouth was trailing her jaw.

She giggled, absolutely content and thoroughly in love. "Well, Mr. Ross, I'm afraid you're gonna have to put that off 'til later." She tugged him down with her to the sofa.

"Much later…"

* * * * *

Two classic Westmoreland novels in one volume!

NEW YORK TIMES BESTSELLING AUTHOR
BRENDA JACKSON
DREAMS OF FOREVER

In *Seduction, Westmoreland Style*, Montana horse breeder McKinnon Quinn is adamant about his "no women on my ranch" rule...but Casey Westmoreland makes it very tempting to break the rules.

Spencer's Forbidden Passion has millionaire Spencer Westmoreland and Chardonnay Russell entering a marriage of convenience... but Chardonnay wants what is strictly forbidden.

"Sexy and sizzling." —*Library Journal* on *Intimate Seduction*

Available July 2012 wherever books are sold.

REQUEST YOUR FREE BOOKS!

2 FREE NOVELS
PLUS 2 FREE GIFTS!

KIMANI™ ROMANCE

Love's ultimate destination!